I0570524

The Daughter's Promise:

A Novella

French Legacy Trilogy Book 1

Rose Pascoe

Published by Flax Bay Books, 2020

Copyright

THE DAUGHTER'S PROMISE
Copyright © 2020 Rose Pascoe.
All rights reserved.

Written by Rose Pascoe
Print on Demand edition September 4, 2024.

This is a work of fiction. Names, characters, places and incidents are either the product of the author's imagination or are used fictionally.

.

ISBN: 978-1067024321

Publisher: Flax Bay Books
Cover design: Rose Pascoe
Cover image by captblack76/Adobe Stock.
Copyediting by Jenny Waters
(www.redheadediting.co.nz)

Contents

Serenity Disturbed

Loire Valley, France, August 1830

Elisabeth Duchamp wandered down the ancient path from the top field, her mind far away, though her feet were sure on the familiar route. Two dairy cows ambling along beside her, snuffling at her fingers and batting their long eyelashes.

A sea of dawn mist filled the valley, leaving them marooned on an island of grass and fruit trees, where the only sounds were the disembodied whistles of the river birds and a startled thrush calling from a hedgerow. From time to time, the wispy grey curtain drifted apart to reveal a glimpse of the Loire River – that always beautiful, but often embattled, dividing line between the north and south of France.

A narrow dirt road wove between the trees along the riverbank, before disappearing into the mist. What would it be like to ride down that road, on and on, until it became wide enough for two carriages to pass with ease, leading eventually to Paris? To leave this secluded valley, her parents, a life she knew and loved?

The thought was not an idle one. Two months ago, when she had turned eighteen, her aunt had written to invite Elisabeth to stay with them in the great City of Light. An opportunity to advance her education and see a little of the wider world. In truth, she yearned to say yes. Had her parents been younger or blessed with more children to help them on the farm, she would be in Paris already. As it was, she was torn between tantalising opportunity and comfortable reality.

Why was it that nobody else had dreams of seeing the world beyond? Claude, the son of a neighbouring dairy farmer, had casually assumed they would marry when she turned eighteen, despite her protests. He had plodded on with an unwavering belief that she would come around, given time, his mind as bovine as his charges. Not that there was anything wrong with him, it simply felt like meekly surrendering before the battle was fought.

Since receiving her aunt's invitation, rumours had begun swirling of further unrest in Paris. If true, the decision might soon be beyond her control.

Marguerite stamped her feet and swished her tail, jolting Elisabeth from her reverie. She found herself in the milking shed, where Marguerite and Brie had taken their usual places and were waiting impatiently for her attention. She settled down on her stool, hitched up her long dress out of the muck, and soon had a stream of warm milk flowing in spurts into the milk pail.

By the time she finished milking, the sun had risen, driving off the mist and turning the river into a wide ribbon of burnished copper. She let the cows out into a nearby field, where a few shoots of green pushed up between the dry stalks left by this hottest of summers. As the cows ambled away together, she leaned her arms on the gate, already warm from the sun.

The tranquillity of the scene should have soothed her, but the sense that change was coming, whether or not she desired it, left her uneasy.

Elisabeth was chiding herself for her overactive imagination when she heard the beat of horse hooves on the road. The trees hid the rider, but he was moving at a steady canter toward their home, so she hurried to close the gate and return to the shed. The milk pails slotted into a handcart, which she pushed up the hill as fast as she could on the stony path.

Halfway up the hill, she heard a loud whoop and spotted a pair of boots dangling from a laden apple tree. 'Hey, monkey-boy, how about picking some of those apples, rather than just enjoying the view?'

The boots did a complete flip around the branch, launching their owner into the air. He somersaulted and landed neatly beside her, catching the three apples he had dislodged as they fell around him, with all the finesse of a juggler. 'I'm too hungry to work.'

Elisabeth noted the tell-tale sign of juice dribbling down his chin and plucked a few stray leaves and twigs from her eleven-year-old nephew's dark mop of rumpled hair. 'François, if you ever said you weren't hungry, I'd collapse in shock. I don't know where you put it all.'

He looked up at her with twinkling hazel eyes and shrugged his bony shoulders. 'Do you think I'll be allowed some cream with breakfast?'

'You might have had cream on apple tart, if you hadn't eaten it all last night.'

'I only had three slices. I'm growing like a weed, according to Grandpapa, so I need lots of extra food.' He put his skinny body to good use by pushing the cart. 'Especially with all this hard work.'

Elisabeth thought his wiry body was more like a sapling tree than a weed – all gangly upward momentum, but with the promise of strength to come. He was dark and lithe, like his father and grandfather, whereas she was fair and blonde, like her mother.

'Elisabeth, did you see the messenger go past? His horse was dripping sweat, so it must be important.'

'Let's find out.' She kept her voice light, though urgent news was seldom good news.

They walked up and over the brow of the hill into the tree-ringed dell where the farmhouse was nestled.

François sniffed the breeze. 'Fresh bread!' He shoved the cart back into her hands and raced on ahead.

Despite the inducement of breakfast and the urgency of the messenger, she felt reluctant to follow him. Instead, she sat down on a smooth slab of limestone, which overlooked the only home she had ever known. Pale limestone walls and a steep, wood-shingled roof, set on a cobbled courtyard. A home to generations of her father's family.

François had almost reached the gate, his skinny legs flailing like a colt let loose in a spring meadow. His high spirits had made him a joy to have around these past six weeks. His father had sent him to help with the fruit harvest, although she suspected her parents were quietly training François to take over her role on the farm, should she decide to go to Paris.

How would her brother cope without his oldest son? Well enough, she thought, as the next oldest was a robust lad, already used to a hard day's work, even though he was only ten years old. Her brother, Henri, was much older than her and had long since married and moved into his own house with his growing family. Only half a day's ride away, but far enough that they did not see each other as often as she would have liked.

Elisabeth closed her eyes, breathing in the heady scents of ripe apples and lavender. A door slammed, rousing her from her daydreaming. No time for that during the harvest season. Especially not when an urgent message had arrived. She rose and headed for the house.

The messenger's horse was in the courtyard, his head down and his coat damp with sweat. She set down the milk pails in the cool of the dairy, before leading the horse towards the barn. Her own horse, Belle, had her head over the fence, inspecting the new arrival with interest. Belle pricked up her ears as her mistress passed, then snorted as she reached the windfall barrel. Elisabeth turned to look into her expressive eyes, prompting Belle to flick her head at the barrel in case she hadn't got the first hint.

Elisabeth relented, as she always did. 'I spoil you, Belle. Soon you'll be too fat to ride.'

Belle snorted again and crunched on her apple with slobbery delight, before kicking up her heels and trotting back across the meadow to the shade of the trees.

Inside, the barn was pleasantly cool, with a comforting smell of fresh hay and ancient wood. The messenger's horse huffed contentedly as he ate the apple and sucked up water from a pail. Elisabeth was about to loosen his girth and rub him down with straw when François appeared, feeding a hunk of bread into a jam-smeared mouth.

'Where have you been, Elisabeth? You're wanted inside.' He jammed the rest of the bread into bulging cheeks as he took the reins from her. 'I'll see to the horse.'

She paused briefly at the water pump to wash her face and hands, then headed inside. After an early start, she was ravenous too, and the thought of a thick slice of her mother's fresh-baked bread with raspberry preserves was as much on her mind as curiosity about the messenger's delivery.

The boy sitting at the table, devouring breakfast, was only a few years older than her nephew and clearly as enthusiastic about food. He looked up at her as she came in – staring, blushing and eating all at the same time. Elisabeth's parents were sitting at the table too, with a leather case between them and worry lines etched on their foreheads. No one spoke until the boy finished eating and rose from the table.

'Your horse is in the barn, watered and fed.' Elisabeth said. 'I wish you a safe return journey.'

The boy gave an awkward bow to each of them and stammered, 'Thank you for your kindness.' He settled his cap back on his head and slipped out the door.

The gnawing sense of unease returned to Elisabeth's belly as she took a seat at the age-scarred wooden table. She helped herself to what remained of the food, while her mother made coffee.

When they were all sitting silently behind steaming cups, Elisabeth raised an eyebrow. 'It's bad news, isn't it?'

Her mother put a thin arm around her shoulders. 'I'm sorry, my dear, but your aunt has sent a letter to say that Paris is in turmoil. You will not be going to stay with her now.'

'Riots and revolt, yet again.' Her father pushed back his chair and began pacing around the kitchen, underscoring his vexation with flailing hands. 'And no wonder. Did the king really think the people would give up their hard-won freedoms without a fight, after all they have suffered?'

'What has happened?' Elisabeth asked.

'The king tried to revoke the Charter!' her father replied, tripping on the hearth and sending a rack of fireirons skittering across the flagstones. He didn't seem to notice the ear-jarring clatter. 'He pays no heed to the rights of the people, which he swore to uphold on his return to the throne. Insanity!'

Elisabeth stared at him in disbelief. 'Surely he will see sense?'

Her parents shook their heads in unison, her father in anger and her mother in despair. Both of her parents had first-hand experience of the horrors of the first revolution. Her mother was more supportive of the legitimist's claim to royal rule, while her father was more sympathetic to rule by the people, but both were realists who understood the precarious balance between peace and anarchy.

They all knew, as apparently the king did not, that attempting to draw away from constitutional rule now was like throwing a cannonball onto the scales on the side of anarchy.

'It is far too late for the king to change his mind,' her mother said, her shoulders sagging under the weight of the news. 'My sister writes that he has been forced to abdicate.'

'Abdicate! Then who sits on the throne now?'

Her mother shook her head, unable to form the words. Seeing her state, her husband enclosed her in his strong arms, gently stroking her hair. When he spoke, his voice was quiet, resignation replacing anger. 'The Duc d'Orléans has seized power by trickery. It seems the king has learned nothing from the chaos of the past forty years.'

'That odious scoundrel, on the throne. The king cannot have forgotten how the Orléans family provoked the first uprising or how the old duke voted for the execution of Louis XVI, his own cousin. Treacherous...' The rest of her mother's sentence was cut short by a chest-rattling bout of coughing.

Elisabeth took her mother's hand, the bony fingers cold and calloused compared to her own. When the fit subsided, she got up to right the fireirons and make her mother a drink of honey and hot water, waiting until she had had a good dose of the soothing liquid, before asking the critical question.

'What news of my aunt?'

'She writes to say they must go into exile in England again. Indeed, she is already on her way to Cherbourg.'

'And the delivery?' Elisabeth gestured to the leather case, which still sat unopened on the far end of the table.

'Your aunt was unable to take her most treasured possessions to England and asked us to hide this until it can be safely returned to her.'

'What is it?'

To Elisabeth's shock, her father slammed his fist down on the table, rattling the cups. She had never seen him like this, so at odds with his normal calm and cheerful nature.

'It is a risk to all of us. After all your so-called aunt put your mother through, I wonder that she has the gall to ask more of her.'

'Calm down, my dear. She suffered more than I did and none of it her own fault. I am sorry to have brought trouble to our door again, but it is too late to send it back now.' Her mother gestured to the case. 'Open it, Elisabeth.'

Elisabeth had watched their interaction with a mixture of fascination and alarm. They rarely argued and never talked of the past. All she had been told was that her mother had been adopted into a wealthy family when she was a young girl, after the death of her own mother, who was their maid. She knew her mother had been treated as a family member and given an education she would never otherwise have had, which explained her fierce loyalty to her adoptive sister.

She wiped her hands and opened the case. It held a stunningly beautiful box of rich, dark wood, inset with an inlaid design in lighter wood around a carved floral centrepiece. The edges of the box were reinforced in gilded metal, embellished with vines and flowers. It was so flawless she could barely bring herself to touch it.

But the desire to see inside was far too strong. With the tips of her fingers, she released the catch and eased the lid open.

The inside was lined with dark blue satin and divided into a number of trays, each fitting perfectly and hinging up to reveal compartments for jewellery. The largest one held an exquisite strand of perfectly matched pearls, while all the other compartments were empty. She let out a breath she hadn't realised she had been holding and looked up at her mother.

'You can see why your aunt would not wish to part with it.' Her mother's gaze kept returning to the jewellery box, with a look of reverence mixed with familiarity. 'This is one of the family heirlooms that I hid for my adoptive family during the revolution. The jewellery box was crafted by the foremost designer in France, Jean Henri Riesener, and is immensely valuable in its own right. The pearl necklace is priceless, to my sister's family at least. And to those who yearn to take it from her.'

Elisabeth could not take her eyes off it. 'Is it safe to have so valuable an item here? Surely it should be locked up somewhere secure?'

'My sister must have had no other choice, especially to entrust it to a messenger. Very few people know of our connection, so perhaps it is as safe here as anywhere. We can hide it in the cheese cave, in case the house is searched.'

Her father snorted. 'And how will that help if someone comes and threatens our children and grandchildren?' The flare of anger burned out quickly as he reached for his wife's hands. 'My darling, you know how ruthless your sister's enemies are.'

'What would you have me do? I don't need to remind you that much of what we have is due to my sister's generosity. Besides, sending it elsewhere would not stop them from coming here.'

Elisabeth took up the jewellery box again and turned it over in her hands. 'Father, could you not make an identical box to give to them if they come?'

Her father's face lit up. 'Brilliant idea, Elisabeth. Thank goodness you inherited your mother's brains as well as her beauty.' He planted an enthusiastic kiss on his wife's cheek. 'I'll get to work straight away. It's such a fine piece of workmanship, I'll need time to get a reasonable likeness.'

'We could put my pearl necklace in the fake box. I would be sorry to lose it, but it might be enough to fool them into thinking it's the real thing.' She turned to Elisabeth. 'It would be best if you hid the gifts you received for your birthday in the real jewellery box too. We cannot afford anything to link us with my sister's family in times like these.'

Elisabeth nodded, although she would be sorry to see her treasures locked away. For her eighteenth birthday, her mother had given her a pair of decorative hair combs, twinkling with tiny diamonds, which had been given to her at the same age. Her aunt had sent her a beautiful cameo brooch, with a head in profile carved in milky-white ivory against a dark blue background, along with the invitation to stay with her in Paris.

Elisabeth could only recall meeting her aunt once in her life, many years ago. She didn't know why her aunt did not visit her mother, as the two sisters had clearly been very close and exchanged letters regularly. Whenever she asked about the past, her mother would grimace for an instant, before the shield went back up. Who cares about the past, she would say, when the present is so delightful? She would sweep Elisabeth into her arms and kiss her face and neck until she dissolved into helpless giggles, making her forget that she'd even asked a question.

Now, as she went up to her room to retrieve the gifts, she thought it fortunate she had not gone to Paris. When she came back down, her father, an expert craftsman, had already begun sketching and measuring the jewellery box. When he had finished the drawing, Elisabeth put her treasures in the box and passed it to her mother, who wrapped it up securely in linen, sealed it in beeswax-lined paper and put it in an old sack.

Her father embraced both women before heading up the path to the caves, whistling as he went. The limestone bluff above the river was peppered with natural caves, whose cool depths were the perfect place to store maturing cheese and wine, as well as fruit and root vegetables for winter. They even grew mushrooms there. The real jewellery box would be safe, even if the fake failed to convince, as there were so many caves it would be impossible to search them all.

Escape

The following three weeks passed quickly. Her father worked long hours in the evening, perfecting the substitute box, while Elisabeth pestered her mother, unsuccessfully, for further information about the heirlooms. After a few days, the jewellery box was forgotten amidst the more urgent demands of fruit-picking, on top of her regular chores.

Their farm was typical of many small-holdings, maintaining an orchard of apples and stone fruit, a couple of dairy cows for milk and cheese, a few pigs and chickens, and a large kitchen garden. They kept what they needed for themselves and sold the rest at the market, or exchanged it for grain, flour and other items they could not grow or make.

Elisabeth had just finished the morning milking, when she heard the ominous drumming of horse hooves on the road. She hustled the cows out into the field and pushed the milk-cart home as fast as she could, with an unsettling sense of déjà vu. The stream of dense smoke issuing from the chimney of the farmhouse did little to calm her nerves. The messenger galloped back past her as she hurried down the path.

As she pushed open the heavy wooden door to the kitchen, she smelled burning rather than the usual welcoming aroma of yeast. Her mother was sitting by the fire, tossing letters into roaring flames. Tendrils of smoke curled up around the pans hanging from a rack on the wall, forming a haze under the rough-sawn timber beams across the kitchen ceiling.

Elisabeth crouched down beside her mother, brushing a stray strand of thin blonde hair out of her flushed face. 'Mother? What is it?'

Her mother threw another handful of letters on the fire. 'It would not be wise to be found with any of your aunt's letters.'

Elisabeth knelt in front of the hearth and poked half-burnt scraps into the flames. She had hoped to read these letters one day, to find out more about her mother's past. She glanced at her mother, seeing red-rimmed eyes and a thin face that was wrinkled beyond her years. Elisabeth knew she and her adoptive family had suffered terribly during the revolution, so these recent events must have rekindled dreadful memories.

As the letters turned to ash, her mother dusted off her hands and turned her back on the burning embers. 'It's just as we feared. We've had an urgent message to warn us that we are no longer safe. Your aunt was searched at Cherbourg and her messenger was forced to reveal where the necklace was taken. You must take the jewellery box to your brother as fast as you can. Your aunt thinks, and your father and I agree, that it would be best if Henri takes it to England, returning it to my sister in person, rather than risk it being found here.'

'But Henri cannot leave his family or his work.'

'We have no choice, my dear.'

'I could go.' She raised a hand to forestall her mother's protests. 'My brother cannot. You know this task must fall to me.'

'No, Elisabeth, it is far too dangerous for you to travel alone.'

'If I don't do this, then none of us will be safe. Besides, I should like to travel to England and meet my aunt. Perhaps Henri could come with me as far as the port, to see me safely onto a ship?'

Her mother hugged her so tightly, Elisabeth could feel her ribs through the layers of clothes. 'It is too much to ask when you are still so young.' Her mother released the embrace and held her at arms-length, searching her face. 'But perhaps you are right. Whoever goes might have to spend days or even weeks in England tracking your aunt down, which would be hard on Henri's family. You may be young, but you are brave. I have great faith in you.'

'I promise to do my best.'

'My darling, you always do. If you are sure you are willing to do this for your family, then you must pack your bags immediately, for we have no time to lose. Take as little as you can, so you can travel quickly. François can go with you back to his house and look after his family, while Henri goes with you to Le Havre.'

'And leave you and Father here alone?' Elisabeth struggled to keep tears from her eyes at the thought of leaving them. Of leaving all of this – her family, her home, her life, and the comfort and security these things represented.

Her mother squeezed her hand. 'Your father and I are too old to travel such a long distance at speed. But we will be safe here until the danger passes. Don't worry, my dear, they will never find our hiding place in the cave.'

She accepted the logic of her mother's words. Her parents were both in their fifties – she had been an unexpected late blessing – and they would be safer once the jewellery box was gone. 'Where is Father? Does he know?'

'He is taking supplies to the cave and retrieving the jewellery box. Come along now, there is much to do.'

Elisabeth hastened up the flight of circular stairs to her bedroom, avoiding the creaks and ducking under the low beam automatically, from years of practice. Sadness welled inside her at the thought this might be the last time she would add her light tread to the smooth dip in the middle of these ancient wooden steps, left by generations of family feet.

She pulled on an old pair of her brother's riding breeches under her loose beige smock and wore her own stout leather boots, knowing from experience that a long horse ride would be agony otherwise. Into the inside of her boot, she slipped a padded sheath holding a small but sharp knife, as a precaution against the brigands who ruled the back roads.

Her packing didn't take long, for they lived a simple life. One good dress for Sunday, two old dresses for work, undergarments, a bonnet and a woollen cloak, along with a scattering of combs, hairpins and handkerchiefs. And lastly, the portrait of her mother as a young girl, which watched over her from the bedside table. A mischievous round face framed with curly blonde hair, just like her own. She hesitated over whether to pack it, but the picture was too precious to leave behind. She wrapped it carefully in a dress and tucked it down the bottom of one pannier, wishing there was a picture of her father to sit beside it.

Finally, a last glance around to check for essentials. She ran her hand over the beautiful quilt, a long-ago gift from her aunt, which was embroidered with pear trees and birds. Her fingers trailed across the short row of precious books, the wooden animals carved by her father, and all the other small treasures she would have to leave behind. She picked out a small but perfect carving of an owl and tucked that away too, to remind her of her father.

Elisabeth had left a space in the panniers for the jewellery box she would carry to England. Her father would bring it back with him, from where it had lain concealed behind the stacks of cheese. He had long ago picked out a cave with a hidden entrance and good ventilation, which would serve the family in times of crisis. It had been crudely furnished and ready for occupation for as long as she could remember.

When she returned to the kitchen, her mother was coming out of the pantry, no doubt checking that the substitute jewellery box was where it should be – sure to be found during a thorough search, but hidden well enough under the jars of preserves to allay suspicion. Her father's carpentry skills had been tested to the limit trying to recreate the perfection of the original Riesener box. Hopefully, it would be enough to convince the searchers.

'All packed?' Her mother handed Elisabeth a drawstring purse, which she tucked into a hidden pocket in her corset. 'If you need any more money, you must sell the cameo and hair-combs.'

'Oh, Mother, I could never sell them. They were gifts.'

'I hope you won't have to, as they are family heirlooms, but you may need to if you have to stay in London for any length of time. They are genuine diamonds, so make sure you get a good price.' Her mother planted a kiss on her forehead. 'François is out in the barn, getting the mare ready. Have a quick breakfast, my love. If your father is not back by the time you have finished, you can loop around by the back path and meet him on the way.'

Elisabeth set to with gusto, knowing she would need the sustenance to get through the long day ahead. 'Don't cry, Mother. With luck, I might only be away a few weeks. I'll be able to practice my English and visit St Paul's Cathedral, to see if it really is bigger than Sainte-Croix d'Orléans.'

Her mother smiled back at her through unshed tears. 'My darling girl, I'll miss you. I know you cannot be so cheerful as you pretend to be. Forgive me, my dear, for putting this burden on your shoulders.'

'There's no real reason to be worried. After all, who would expect a young farm girl to be carrying such valuables? I'll deliver the necklace as promised, family honour will be satisfied, and I'll be back before you know it, to enjoy the last of the season's apples. If François hasn't eaten them all first.'

Her mother reached out and clutched her hand tightly. 'Just remember what I taught you. You may not be physically strong enough to overcome an adversary, but there is always a way out of any situation if you stay calm and use your ingenuity.

And remember, no piece of jewellery, no matter how valuable, is worth more than your own life.'

Her father had not arrived back by the time she finished, so they went out, arm-in-arm, to the grey stone barn, where François was waiting with Belle. The mare gave a low nicker at her arrival and pushed her muzzle into Elisabeth's hand, crunching down on the piece of carrot she knew would be there.

Belle had been Elisabeth's horse to care for and train ever since she was a tiny filly with twigs for legs. She was now a sturdy six-year-old, strong enough to carry both Elisabeth and François as far as Henri's farm. Elisabeth strapped her panniers to the back of the saddle and checked that her nephew's small bundle was slung over his back. The moment she was dreading had arrived. She wrapped her arms around her mother and kissed her cheeks.

Her mother hugged her tightly, then gently extricated herself and dabbed at both of their tear-stained faces with her apron. She handed Elisabeth a piece of paper with a name and address on it. 'I do not know where your aunt will be, but she and I will send messages to you at this address in London.'

'Mr Arthur Postlethwaite,' she read, stumbling over the impossible English name, 'Dealer in Antiquarian Books.' She tucked the paper into the lining of her corset. 'He is not French?'

'No, but your aunt says he has helped before and is completely trustworthy.'

Elisabeth mounted Belle. 'Goodbye, Mother. Stay safe. I'll write when I arrive and come back just as soon as I can.'

Her mother gripped her leg tightly. 'No, my dear Elisabeth, you must stay in England and promise not contact us until I send word that it is safe to return. If you cannot find your aunt, try to get work as a governess until one of us sends a message. You'll have to be brave, my darling daughter.'

'But what if something goes wrong and I don't hear from you?'

'Of course you will hear from us.' Her mother attempted a light laugh, which entirely failed to convince her daughter. She turned to her grandson, who had been standing quietly beside Belle, stroking the mare's nose. 'Goodbye, François. Tell your father to make sure your family leaves the farm until we send word.'

He hugged her tightly, wordlessly, then vaulted onto Belle from behind. They walked out across the cobbled yard with bowed heads, in silence, apart from the clopping of hooves and the buzzing of bees around the peach trees. When they reached the gate, Elisabeth turned to wave, but her mother was already hurrying inside, her retreating shadow shimmering in the intense summer heat.

They met her father less than half a mile down the path, with a sack over his shoulder. Both of them jumped off Belle and raced to embrace him. He picked them up in turn, with arms strengthened by a lifetime of outdoor work, and whirled them around, as he used to do when they were little children. 'How did you both grow so big without me noticing?' He planted a stubbly kiss on Elisabeth's cheek.

'Papa, I am to take the necklace to England.' She watched for his reaction, expecting a refusal, but he simply sighed, as if it was what he had been expecting, and whirled her again. 'Papa, enough, or I'll be sick.'

'I will miss you, my girl.'

'Not as much as I will miss you. Who will teach me about plants and animals and the wonders of the world?'

Her father wrapped the sacking tighter around the jewellery box and handed it to Elisabeth. 'I'm sure you'll meet many folks who know a lot more about those things than me. And you'll be travelling further that I have ever done in my whole life. Think what wonders you will see with your own eyes. I look forward to hearing every detail when you return.'

Elisabeth slipped the box deep into the pannier and tucked some of her undergarments over it, hoping they might be enough to dissuade any inspection by the new king's soldiers. She tried to match his light tone. 'I'm only going to England, not travelling the mighty oceans fighting off gigantic sea monsters or crossing jungles infested with snakes and tigers.'

'I am relieved to hear it.' He kissed her forehead, then turned his eyes away. 'You're stronger than you realise, my dearest Elisabeth, just like your mother. I know you will come through this. And we will be waiting here for your return, when things have settled down again. We've been through worse troubles than this and survived.'

Elisabeth was too choked up to say anything else, as she clung to him one last time.

'Look!' cried François, pointing down the valley.

Three powerful horses were cantering along the riverside road, kicking up puffs of dust at each hoof-beat. Each was carrying a man whose upright posture and dangling sword labelled him as a soldier – or one of the legions of ex-soldiers turned mercenary. As they watched, the trio turned up the track towards the farmhouse.

'Get on the horse and go. Now! You can go down the side-track and cut behind them without being seen.' Her father lingered only long enough to see them both on Belle, before he slapped the horse's rump hard.

The mare jumped forward with a start and cantered down the path. Elisabeth hung on to her mane while she got her feet back in the stirrups and gathered the reins. By the time she had Belle back under control, her father was halfway up the hill, running for the house as if the devil was chasing him.

'Elisabeth, stop, we have to go back.' François was tugging at her waist, his voice high with panic.

'No, François, I promised I'd get you to safety.'

'We can't just leave them with three armed soldiers.'

Their fear was upsetting Belle, who skittered and danced across the track, on the edge of a steep bank. Elisabeth pulled Belle to a halt and calmed her down with long strokes on her silky neck. She needed to calm herself down too, to decide whether to obey her parents' explicit orders or give in to the urgent desire to help them.

She pointed to a small copse of trees nearby. 'You wait there with Belle. I'll go back.'

He shot her a look she had seen a hundred times on the menfolk of her family. No way was he leaving her to fight alone.

'All right, I get it. Let's go.' They galloped back up the hill as fast as Belle could go. Elisabeth reined her in as they approached the crest of the hill. 'No point rushing in without a plan.'

She tethered Belle out of sight, with enough free rein that she could rest and crop some grass.

They left her there and sidled through the belt of trees ringing the meadow around the house.

Elisabeth could see her father, halfway across the meadow and heading for the house, and heard him calling out to her mother. Her mother appeared in the doorway, took in her husband's urgency, and started running across the courtyard. Thank goodness, she thought, they are going to get away before the soldiers arrive.

But her hope was shattered by the appearance of three men coming around the bend and down into the dell. They were not in uniform, but there was no mistaking their military bearing and weaponry. They must have tethered their horses in the trees to give them the advantage of surprise.

Their leader yelled and pointed in the direction of the fleeing couple. All three of them changed direction and raced after her parents. They were too young and fit – her parents were not going to make it even as far as the edge of the meadow.

She could sense the boy beside her getting ready to spring into attack. She grabbed his arm, pulling him down behind the bushes. 'We can't fight off three armed men. We'll have to wait and rescue them while the soldiers are searching the house.'

'They might be killed.'

'Not before the soldiers get what they want.'

As if to confirm her desperate logic, the leader shouted, 'Take them alive.'

At that moment, her mother made the mistake of looking back. Her foot caught on something, and she fell heavily to the ground. Her father turned to pull her up, but it was too late. One of the soldiers bowled him over and trapped him on the ground, while the other held a sword to her mother's throat. The leader, who was built for power rather than speed, reached them seconds later. He tossed a handful of leather ties to each man and ordered them to bind their hands behind their backs.

The captives were taken back to the house and tied to the water pump in the courtyard, one on each side. The leader gestured towards the house and barn, sending his two men off in separate directions.

Elisabeth leaned over to whisper in her nephew's ear. 'I'll try to cut them free. You get their horses and be ready to bring them down behind the barn, close enough for us to mount up and escape.' It wasn't much of a plan, but she could think of no other. 'And François, if anything goes wrong, it'll be your responsibility to ride as fast as you can to your father. He'll know what to do.'

She could sense him hesitating and realised what he was thinking. With his smaller size, they might have a better chance of success if he was the one to sneak across the courtyard. She looked back at him, unblinking. He took off his dull brown cap and held it out to her. She smiled and slipped it on, tucking all traces of her distinctive blonde hair under its rim. Just as well he had a big head on his slim body. François reached around to tuck in a final stray stand, nodded and disappeared without a sound.

Down in the courtyard, Elisabeth saw the two soldiers reappear and heard them call out an 'all clear'. She slithered her way down and around the slope between the trees until she reached the shelter of the barn, which was close to the water pump. She could hear the leader questioning her mother in the strident voice of a man used to giving orders and having them obeyed, but she couldn't hear her mother's quiet replies.

Elisabeth picked up a broken piece of heavy railing, crept around to the far end of the barn, where a stack of hay gave her some cover, and peeped through the wispy stems at the edge.

The leader – an enormous bear of a man – thrust the tip of his sword to within a finger's breadth of her mother's nose. 'You know what I am here for. Give it to me and I will let you live.'

Her mother did not even flinch as she calmly replied, 'You think I trust you? I know you will kill me anyway, so why would I give you anything?'

He twirled the sword, so the sunlight flashed off it into her face with each turn. 'Why? Perhaps because you would not wish to see your husband lose his fingers. One by one.' His block of a face

33

betrayed no emotion, as if this type of threat was a mundane task for him, though his dark eyes shone with relish.

Elisabeth heard her mother's sharp intake of breath.

Her father, who was trying to fray the cord tying his hands by rubbing it against the hard edge of the pump, hissed, 'Don't tell him anything.'

But the threat was too much for her mother. 'It's in the kitchen.'

The leader strode off towards the house. After a moment's silence, the air filled with the sound of crockery smashing on the flagstone floor.

Across the courtyard, a sudden squawking drew the attention of the two guards. A dozen hens burst out of their coop, followed by the tabby cat. The hens dashed about in all directions, creating mayhem, before they escaped under the fence. The cat licked its paws and settled back into a sunny nook as if nothing had happened.

Clever lad, François, Elisabeth thought, as she used his distraction to get her father's attention. She held up her knife and the pitchfork she had taken from the haystack. He blinked at her twice, so she slithered across the open courtyard to the water pump. It was too narrow to hide her completely, but both the soldiers were still staring at the other side of the courtyard to see what had frightened the hens, confident that their prisoners could not escape.

Inside the kitchen, a resounding clash of metal told her that their leader had pulled the rack of pots off the wall. They had no more than a minute or two before he discovered the door to the pantry. As she severed her father's ties, she saw the two soldiers suddenly sprinting towards the open door of the barn. Over her father's shoulder, she caught a glimpse of her nephew, waving his arms and legs like a manic puppet. As she watched, horrified, François dashed into the barn with the soldiers in pursuit.

'François is trapping them in the barn,' her father whispered. 'Quick, we have to bar the door.'

Elisabeth sliced through the last of his bindings, then freed her mother's hands and left the knife for her to free her feet. Her father was already halfway to the barn, in which she could hear shouting and a sudden crashing. François must have made it to the loft and thrown down the ladder. Her father was at the thick wooden door now, heaving it into place and slotting down the solid wooden bar, sealing the soldiers in.

In the kitchen, the shattering of preserving jars signalled that their attacker was about to reach his target.

'Get out of here, now!' her father yelled to her, as he headed back across the courtyard.

Elisabeth jumped the fence and raced around the side of the barn to fasten the shutters on the single small window. The soldiers were now locked in, at least until they could batter their way out through the door, which had stood firm against storms for more than a century.

Above her were the only other windows, which were little more than ventilation slits in the stone wall. A tousled mop of hair appeared, followed by a writhing body, miraculously squeezing through the impossibly narrow gap. François twisted himself around and flipped to the ground, landing neatly at her feet with a wide grin on his face.

She hugged him tightly for a moment. 'Go get those horses, monkey-boy, as fast as you can.' She risked a quick look around the corner of the barn, to make sure her parents were safe, just as the lead soldier ran out of the house, carrying the fake jewellery box. He had to put it down so he could draw his sword, which gave her parents the extra second needed to spin around and face him. He advanced on them across the courtyard, calling for his men and swinging the heavy sword with practiced ease.

Her father moved in front of her mother, the pitchfork swinging in defiance of the blade. Her mother still had the knife in her hand, its feeble blade looking tiny against the huge sword. Elisabeth looked around desperately for a weapon, but could do no better than a couple of loose stones. Behind her, she heard the sound of a single set of hooves approaching, barely discernible over the hammering of the soldiers on the barn door. She glanced behind, fearing another soldier, but it was only Belle, who must have got loose and come in search of her.

Her mother was speaking. 'You have what you want. Leave us be and take it far away from here. I'll be pleased to see it gone.'

'You think I can't take on two old crones with a pitchfork and a butter knife? My orders were to find the jewellery box and leave no witnesses.'

He advanced, flicking his blade to block her father's thrusting pitchfork, spinning it out of his hands. Elisabeth threw her stones with all her might. The first one went wide, but distracted the soldier for an instant, while the second stone caught him a glancing blow on the brow. As the soldier grunted and turned to find his unexpected attacker, she saw her mother dash forward with the knife.

The soldier's quick reflexes saved him, knocking the knife away from his heart, diverting the momentum of her mother's lunge upward. The knife sliced his cheek from mouth to eye. He roared in anger and thrust his sword at her, catching the edge of her arm. A bright red line appeared and the knife clattered to the ground.

Her father had picked up the pitchfork again, but Elisabeth didn't wait around to watch the inevitable. She ran to Belle and swung into the saddle. With one hand on the panniers, pulling out the sack with the jewellery box, and one hand on the reins, she urged her horse forward with her legs and voice. Undergarments and dresses scattered in all directions as Belle galloped forward a dozen strides, then jumped the fence.

The soldier froze in place, watching wide-eyed as Belle's muscled body charged towards him. He tried to leap aside at the last second, but Elisabeth was already twirling the sack, catching him on the side of the head and felling him like a rotten tree whose time had come. Belle skidded to a halt at the far side of the yard, her nostrils quivering with the sudden exertion. Elisabeth patted her neck and whispered her thanks into a hairy ear, which twitched at the praise.

Her parents were standing with their mouths open. Her father broke the trance first, ripping the arm off his shirt to tie around his wife's arm, before tying up the unconscious soldier. Elisabeth rushed inside for a proper bandage, honey, and a basin of warm water.

Belle thrust her nose over Elisabeth's shoulder as she helped her father to clean the wound. Fortunately, it was superficial, although it must have been extremely painful. A couple of inches to the side, and the sword would have sliced through an artery.

François was racing towards the yard, dwarfed by the three horses trailing behind him. 'Wooah, that was amazing, Aunt Elisabeth! I didn't know Belle could jump like that.'

'I'm not sure she knew it either,' Elisabeth said, and suddenly she was laughing and hugging her beloved horse, who merely snorted and fluttered her long eyelashes. She left Belle to wander over to the trough and sample the hay, while she finished smearing the cut with honey and bandaging it. Her mother, typically, ignored the wound, and focussed on praising the actions of her daughter and grandson.

Her father was as practical as ever. 'I hate to break up this happy reunion, but we need to get moving. Sounds like the barn door won't hold much longer.'

He helped his wife to mount gentle Belle, while François transferred the panniers to one of the soldiers' horses and Elisabeth gathered up her scattered clothes, her knife and the sack holding the jewellery box. Her father was halfway across the meadow, leading Belle, by the time François and Elisabeth had mounted two of the soldier's horses and followed them, with the third horse tossing its head behind them on a lead rein. They left to the sound of the two soldiers hollering and battering repeatedly at a broken slat in the door. The fake jewellery box lay where it had been dropped, beside the still-unconscious body of the massive soldier.

They rode out together until they reached the track to the caves. François stayed with the horses, while Elisabeth got down and tied a leafy branch to Belle's tail, so that her hoof marks would be obscured on the dusty trail, as she took her parents into hiding. Belle flicked her tail once, but accepted this outrage with good grace. Elisabeth went around to stroke her nose one last time.

Her father put one arm around her shoulders, which had begun to shake with the delayed shock of their narrow escape. 'You shouldn't have come back for us, though I'm glad you did. I'm so proud of you both for your courage and cleverness. And Belle too. We'll look after her for you, my dearest daughter.' He kissed her cheek. 'Time to go now and not look back.'

She hugged him tightly. Her mother looked down on them with a smile on her lips, but her pale face and trembling hands showed how fragile she was feeling. Elisabeth smiled back and held her mother's hand for a moment, telling herself that her mother would be fine in her father's tender care. They had loved each other for over forty years and still exchanged fond glances and kisses like a couple of newlyweds. That was the kind of love Elisabeth hoped for too, if fate was on her side.

Her father gathered up Belle's reins and they headed down the track. Her mother looked back once and waved before they disappeared around a bend.

Elisabeth and François set off at a fast walk down the back path to the river, keeping their thoughts to themselves, until they reached a dip in the track. Here, she allowed the dam of tears to burst, giving herself over completely to grief for a precious minute. François rode on silently beside her, his own body shaking with barely suppressed shock. Without a word, they pressed the horses into a steady canter, not looking back.

They rode on along the riverside road, walking the horses when they tired, stopping briefly for a rest in a dense stand of trees, reaching her brother's house well before the afternoon sun dipped behind the hills.

Their tale was left until later that evening, after François' younger siblings were in bed. His mother, Mathilde, who grew up in a normal farming family, went from raised eyebrows, to gasps, and finally to shocked exclamations as the story unfolded. His father, Henri, was no longer surprised by anything his parents did, merely shaking his head and proudly praising his son's bravery and cunning.

'So, my dear sister, what now? Time to retreat? Or take on the entire French army?'

Elisabeth was grateful for Henri's return to practical matters. Despite the fifteen-year age gap between them, he had always treated her with kindness and respect. 'Mother and Father said your family should stay with Mathilde's relatives for a while until these men are well out of the way.'

'And you?'

'Carry on as planned. I'll travel to Le Havre and find a ship bound for England. I think it might be safer to continue dressed as a boy, if François will let me keep his cap.'

'Perhaps you should use a different name too,' Mathilde suggested, 'in case they send men to the ports to look for you.'

'But not too different or I might not react when I hear it.'

'How about Duval?' François suggested. 'Elisabeth of the Valley has a nicer ring to it than Elisabeth of the Field.'

Elisabeth tried the name out in her mind and liked it. 'How about Elise Duval? I'll use it if I need to send a message. François, will you tell your grandparents?'

'Of course, Aunt Elise. Or perhaps it should be Uncle Elie, if you're to be a boy.'

Mathilde got up and started clearing the table. 'There's a lot to do if we're going away. François, you will have to take the cows over to our neighbour tomorrow. The chickens can run loose in the garden for a few days.'

Elisabeth rose too, suddenly feeling overwhelmed with exhaustion. 'It'll be an early start in the morning for me too.'

'I will be coming with you.' Henri saw her hesitation. 'I insist. Travelling alone is dangerous for anyone these days, let alone a young woman. I would never forgive myself if anything happened to you. François can be the man of the family for a couple of weeks.'

Her nephew straightened his back. 'I won't let them come to any harm, Father. But I will miss you, Aunt Elisabeth. Please don't stay away long.'

'I'll do my best. I'll miss you too, monkey-boy.' And she would. François was more like a brother to her than a nephew, and his sense of fun kept her spirits up. She kissed him on the cheek and for once he didn't squirm away.

The next morning, she and Henri left well before the rooster roused himself to welcome the dawn, taking the three soldiers' horses with them. They swapped the distinctive military saddles and bridles for ordinary tack and roughened up the horses' coats with mud to disguise their fine breeding. The military-issue gear disappeared into the deepest part of the Loire River as they crossed the bridge and headed north at a steady canter.

They pressed on at a gruelling pace, day after day, travelling light, resting regularly and swapping between their mounts to keep them fresher. Once, they heard the drumming of hoofbeats behind them and only just had time to hide in the trees as a group of soldiers thundered past. They appeared intent only on the road ahead, but Elisabeth's heart buzzed as erratically as a fly in a bottle for at least ten minutes after they had passed.

Several small bands of ruffians, loitering in the trees by the path, posed a greater threat, but the sight of three powerful horses surging past at a brisk pace was enough to dissuade them from any ill-intent. Still, Elisabeth was glad to have Henri at her side, both on the road and when it came to negotiating a room at an inn each night. She hunched down in her over-sized coat and attended to the horses, without saying a word to anyone besides Henri, and tried not to dwell on her gross lack of experience in the world beyond their farm.

Their relentless flight north kept her numb in the saddle and exhausted by dark, which was all to the good, as it helped her to push away the worry she felt for her parents and Henri's family. All she could do now was pray they were safe and the soldiers had returned to their master in disgrace. Instead, she passed the time conjuring happy thoughts of her parents sitting side-by-side in the cheese cave, sipping wine and nibbling cheese by candlelight, telling stories to each other.

Henri sold one horse at Lisieux, another just before they crossed the Seine River, and the last on the approach to Le Havre, thinking it best not to draw attention to themselves by selling three prime battle horses in a single market. They fetched a good price. Henri pressed most of the money into Elisabeth's hands, keeping some aside to buy a nondescript bay mare for the return journey.

They carried on to the port, walking and riding alternately. As they passed each milestone, the knot in Elisabeth's gut grew tighter, as the time to leave France drew closer.

The knot was all but forgotten on reaching Le Havre, as the parade of new sights captivated her. The town itself was bustling with all manner of strange-looking people, talking in languages Elisabeth did not recognise. And so many buildings, both grand and modest, with several charming streets lined with tall, narrow buildings jammed together like an uneven row of books. But it was the sight of the sea, sand and sailing ships that left them both open-mouthed in wonder.

The port, sited at the mouth of the Seine, was a forest of masts sprouting from a mass of ships, large and small, amidst a frenzy of activity. One vessel had the most extraordinary chimney on it, twice as tall as an apple tree, belching smoke. It moved rapidly up the river, despite not having any sails. A passer-by told them it was a steam-powered ship, which took passengers and cargo to Paris. If only her father had been there to see such a marvel. She filed the image into her memory, hoping to share it with him soon.

Darkness had closed in on them by the time they found an inn near the port that looked respectable, amidst the many catering to drunken sailors and ladies of dubious morals. Elisabeth hardly slept a wink, partly because of the loud revelry in the street and partly because of the mix of excitement and dread within her.

For the next two days, Henri did the rounds of shipping agents, looking for a safe berth to England, with no success. Elisabeth was happy to sit high in the attic room of the inn, resting her aching muscles and watching the ships come in, unload and depart again, their many sails billowing as they disappeared to a far blue horizon.

Soon, she would experience for herself the feeling of being pushed by the wind across that endless expanse of water, afloat in a glorified wooden barrel. She could only pray that Henri would find a ship that wasn't populated with the likes of the vile-smelling drunkards who gathered under her window, singing through the night in strange languages and lunging with raucous laughter at any woman who was foolish enough to walk by.

Farewell to France

Early on the third day, she heard Henri's light step on the narrow stairs. He brought breakfast and possible good news.

'The innkeeper says an English ship arrived yesterday, belonging to a trustworthy man of his acquaintance. They'll be returning to London later today. He only takes cargo, not passengers, but I hope to persuade him to make an exception for you. I have to say that I have not been impressed by the calibre of the men I have met here. Perhaps I should come with you.'

Elisabeth felt a surge of hope that he would, but said nothing. After all, she was dressed as a boy and was carrying a sharp knife – what harm could come to her if she stayed in her cabin and spoke as little as possible?

Henri was gone all morning, returning in the early afternoon with a young man who was tall enough to have to duck under the low lintel, but of slim build. 'May I present Mr John Godwin? This is my … my brother, Elie Duval. Mr Godwin owns a ship leaving for England this afternoon.'

The man removed his hat and bowed. '*Bonjour*. Your brother tells me he will pay me well to deliver a valuable package to London.' His French was passable and his manner polite, but his tone remained cautious.

'You may speak English, if you please,' Henri said. 'We are both fluent. May I offer you some refreshment?' Henri disappeared before hearing his answer, leaving behind an awkward silence.

Mr Godwin appraised her with the air of one who does not miss much. 'Would I be right in guessing that you are the package? We get many requests from people wanting to leave France, but you must understand it creates problems with the authorities that I would much rather avoid.'

'You are correct, Mr Godwin. I wish to leave France as soon as possible, without attracting attention on myself,' she replied in what she hoped was correct, if accented, English. 'I apologise for the waste of your time.'

His relentless study of her face continued. 'As it happens, I do have a very small cabin that I could make available. As a gentleman, I am compelled to consider your safety, as I would not wish to see you come to harm.'

Elisabeth sat silently, assessing the man across the table. He had an honest, down-to-earth look about him. His light brown hair was cut simply and his clothes were practical rather than flashy – a tailored coat that was thinning around the elbows and cuffs, a plain waistcoat and cravat, trousers made of some tough material, with streaks of dirt and tar, and a pair of sturdy boots. His face was all angles and by no means handsome, but he had crinkles of good humour around his soft brown eyes, which looked on her with a kindness that reminded her of Belle.

'Mademoiselle Duval, I suggest you tuck that stray lock of hair under your cap, if you wish to travel as a lad,' he said with calm nonchalance, indicating with a tap on his neck where the hair had fallen.

'Thank you, Mr Godwin.' She attempted to mirror his casual manner as she tucked up the wayward strand, but the effect was ruined by the blush spreading across her face and neck. What hope did she have if her disguise had been seen through so easily? 'I would be very grateful to accept your offer. I hope I do not cause you a problem.'

'I'm sure it will be fine.' He leaned forward and raised an eyebrow. 'As long as you are not a dangerous criminal wishing to escape justice.'

She was about to respond with a fervent denial, but she saw from the quirk of his lips that he was only jesting. 'I assure you that you will be safe from me, Mr Godwin.

'I'm glad to hear it.' He laughed, breaking the remaining tension and making him look younger and less severe.

With a jolt of surprise, she realised he was not much older than herself. 'Shall I call you Captain?'

'Mr is fine. I am the owner of the ship and most often to be found in my office in London, which is where my captains prefer me. But I like to sail as often as I can, to keep an eye on our ships and trading conditions.' He rocked back on the chair and studied her. 'You have not been to London before, I assume?'

'No, I have not travelled beyond Orléans, but I have heard that London is a vast city with more than a million of citizens. I look forward to seeing it.'

'You have family or friends there to stay with?'

'I wish to find a relative who went to England. And to improve my English while I am there. I will look for a position as a governess, if I need to stay for some time.'

'May I say your English is already excellent. Far better than my French.' He leaned forward with his elbows on the table, his chin cupped in his hands. 'I can see you have been well educated. May I ask if you have any experience as a governess?'

'I speak French, English and German and have studied history, science and mathematics, but I have no training as a teacher, nor much talent at the finer arts, such as music and needlework.'

Henri returned, followed by the innkeeper, who was balancing a tray with a carafe of wine, three glasses, plates and an assortment of cheeses and bread. The innkeeper broke into a wide smile when he saw Mr Godwin, welcoming him back to France with a hearty clap on the back.

Elisabeth took it as a good sign, suggesting that Mr Godwin was an honest man who paid his bills and caused no disruption. Judging from the sounds of drunkenness and brawling she had heard on the previous two nights in the streets of Le Havre, such good behaviour was a rare commodity.

When the innkeeper left the room, Elisabeth caught Henri's eye as he poured the wine. 'Mr Godwin was not deceived by my disguise, but he has kindly agreed to take me to England.'

Henri raised his glass. 'I am very grateful to you, sir. To your very good health, Mr Godwin, and a safe voyage.'

'Thank you for your hospitality. I was about to tell Mademoiselle Duval that I have a sister, aged twelve, who is in need of an intelligent companion and much more interested in history and science than embroidery. I was wondering if perhaps she would care to stay with us as our guest for a few days on arrival? If the arrangement is suitable to all parties, perhaps she might stay on with Anne for as long as she cares to. We have plenty of spare room in the house.'

Relief surged through her at the thought of having a place to stay, at least for the first few days. Elisabeth had a strong feeling that John Godwin was a decent man and, from the relief on Henri's face, he felt the same. She nodded at Henri, and the two men shook hands to confirm the arrangement. Under the circumstances, they felt no need for

Henri to accompany her to London, especially as they were both keen for him to return to his family and parents.

Late that afternoon, Mr Godwin called to collect her. They pushed through a crowd of sailors, dockworkers, horses, carts and barrows, until they reached the far end of the wharf.

'There she is,' he said, pointing to a two-masted sailing ship, which was being loaded with barrels and crates. 'She may not be as fast as some, but her broad beam makes for smooth sailing. We'll be casting off soon. That'll be the last of the cargo, and the tide has already turned.'

Henri followed them down on horseback. They had already shared an emotional farewell in the privacy of their room at the inn, so she tried not to look back at him. He waited until she was on board before waving and turning his new horse to the road home.

She pulled her cap down further, surreptitiously brushing away a tear, and concentrated on gritting her teeth and following the slim figure of Mr Godwin as he made his way across the cluttered deck with practised ease. The ship rolled under her feet, making her weave slightly from side to side. To her surprise, it wasn't an unpleasant sensation – more like a rocking chair than a bucking horse.

Mr Godwin introduced her to the captain as 'Master Duval, son of a friend'. The captain merely grunted a greeting and continued preparing the ship to sail. A few of the sailors gave her a cursory glance before turning back to their tasks. She followed Mr Godwin below the rear deck, where he showed her a tiny cabin.

'It might be best if you stay in the cabin as much as possible. My apologies for the lack of comfort.'

'It is more than adequate, thank you, Mr Godwin. Please, do not let me keep you from your duty.'

The cabin looked as if it was rarely used, except as a store room, with barely room to stand beside the narrow bunk, even for someone as small as her. But it was clean and safe, which was all she wanted. She had switched her possessions from the saddlebags to a battered old canvas sack, which her brother had bought at the market. This she tucked into a dark corner, under a pile of sailcloth, behind a stack of wooden boxes with labels from Normandy. The boxes smelled of cheese, which was a very pleasant aroma indeed compared to the smell of tar and damp wood that pervaded the rest of the ship. Overhead, she could hear the crew preparing for departure.

Her breath caught in her throat as a booming French voice overrode the English commands, followed by the thump of heavy boots on the gangplank. She was trying to decide between brazening it out or finding a hiding place, when there was a sharp rap on the door. Her heart pounded as she opened it, but it was not a soldier, only a sailor who looked to be made almost entirely of wiry sinew and grey hair.

He handed her a seaman's cap and a jacket stiff with salt and grease. 'Mr Godwin says we must hide you, lass, and be quick about it. He suggested the sail locker, but you'd be safer aloft, if you've a head for heights. Nobody ever looks up.'

'Up it is then.' She pulled on the foul jacket and checked her hair was completely covered by the cap, praying that it did not infest her with lice. Although lice would be the least of her problems if she was caught.

The man made no comment, other than to introduce himself with a gruff, 'Rivers, mate'. He led her forward under the deck, hobbling with a stiff gait and a grimace through packed rows of cargo, until they came to a hatch near the front mast. Elisabeth scrambled up the rope netting to the first spar, where she crouched behind a bulging roll of canvas. From her perch, she could see two men following Mr Godwin to the rear of the ship – a port inspector and a soldier by the looks of them.

As she watched them disappear below deck, a cascade of canvas dropped from the spar above her and a gravelly voice yelled at her to 'get a move on'. By the time she'd struggled with the salt-stiff bindings – thankful for her strong fingers from

54

years of milking – and unfurled her section of sail, the men had left the ship.

With a few stentorian commands and a synchrony of movement, the sailors set about casting off the thick mooring ropes and working the winches.

Out of the shelter of the harbour, a gusty breeze caught the sails and punched them into a taunt arc. For the first time in her life, Elisabeth experienced the raw power of a ship under canvas. She was still sitting on the spar, clinging to the mast and grinning at the thrill of racing across wind-whipped waves, when Mr Godwin called up from the base of the mast. She climbed back down to the deck beside him.

'The mate, Mr Rivers, told me where you were, but I didn't believe him. Never had a woman up the rigging before.'

'Wonderful view from up there.'

He shook his head and laughed. 'You looked like you were enjoying it.'

'It was exhilarating, like galloping on a horse, but across the sea. My father would be marvelling at the power of the wind, controlled by something as small as a person.'

'Perhaps I should offer you a job on the crew.'

'I'm not sure the crew would want that. Is it not bad luck to have a woman on a ship?' Her smile dropped away as she turned to him. 'Thank you for hiding me. You took a big risk.'

He waved the thanks away. 'Dealing with the ever-increasing demands of these port officials is getting tedious. We'd already had the cargo inspected and all our papers checked. There was no need for them to check again.'

'Did they say what they were looking for?' She thought it unlikely that the soldiers who had attacked their house in the Loire Valley could have followed them as far as Le Havre, without their horses and with no idea of which way to go. But she wasn't willing to take any risks.

'Only for undocumented passengers. There are always people at the ports trying to escape France. They know we only carry cargo, so they don't bother us as a rule. But I'd have to say they searched much more thoroughly than usual, as if they really thought someone was being concealed aboard. It's just as well you didn't hide in the sail locker. I'd swear my heart stopped beating when they insisted on checking in there.'

'Then I am even more grateful that you agreed to take me. I must return to the cabin, so as not to cause a problem.'

'Don't worry about the crew – they're all old hands and loyal to the company. Ask Rivers if you need anything – he's a good man. Started out as a cabin boy for my father before I was born.'

She was content to lie down on her narrow bunk and rest, but the rocking motion and the rhythmic whoosh of the waves on the hull, only a few inches away from her ears, sent her into a deep sleep. When a rap at the door wakened her, she had no idea of the time, except that it was pitch dark outside the grimy porthole.

'Master Duval? Would you care to join me for supper?'

For a second, the name did not register in her sleep-addled brain. Life would be so much easier when she went back to being Elisabeth Duchamp, she thought, as she opened the door. 'Thank you, Mr Godwin.' Her stomach growled its appreciation, having not been fed since breakfast.

He stared at her as if she was a creature risen from the depths of the ocean. 'I beg your pardon. It's just ... your hair ... however did you fit it all under that cap?'

She reached a hand up. Her hair had come loose as she slept and had bunched up into a tangled pouf. With a sigh, she plaited the exuberant curls tightly, pinning the plait up and shoving the cap on top.

He suppressed a smile, adding, 'The waves are not making you feel unwell, I hope?'

'Not at all. I was just tired.'

'That's grand. Most first-timers, and many old hands, get terribly seasick crossing the English Channel. Follow me.'

He led the way to a cabin at the back end of the ship, or stern, as he called it. It was more spacious that her cabin – big enough for a small desk and table, both heaped with papers. There was a tray on the floor with two tin bowls of unidentifiable brown slurry and a plate with hunks of baguette. Mr Godwin swept up the papers from the table and dumped them on the only other available space, a bunk as narrow and short as hers. He must have to sleep with his knees around his ears.

He lifted the two bowls to the table, sniffing at the contents with a dubious twist of his nostrils. 'Sorry I woke you up for this, Mademoiselle … I mean, Master Duval. I'm finding it hard to keep it straight in my mind.'

'You may call me as you wish, Mr Godwin. You need not talk at all if it makes you uncomfortable.'

'I fear I did not think the matter through when I agreed to take you. I cannot offer a married lady as chaperone, but perhaps you would prefer to have Mr Rivers join us?'

Elisabeth glanced around the cabin, which was hardly large enough for two to dine in. 'Perhaps it would be best to think of me as the son of a friend. Or I could eat in my cabin.'

'Truth is, I like a bit of conversation and get tired of talking about cargo from dawn 'til dusk. Eat up, you must be starving.'

Elisabeth was hungry enough to eat anything, which was just as well. After a mouthful or two, she hazarded a guess that it might be a beef stew, but with far too much salt and no herbs or vegetables at all. 'May I have some water?'

'Good idea.' He poured two mugs of water from a jug. 'Perhaps you would care for some wine to wash this slop down?'

'That would be appreciated, thank you.'

The burgundy – in a proper glass – was as excellent as the food was awful. By taking a sip after each mouthful, she found the meal almost palatable, even if it meant drinking more than she was accustomed to.

Mr Godwin pushed away his empty bowl with the look of man relieved to have an unpleasant chore over. 'I really must find a new cook before the men mutiny. How about a bit of decent cheese to take away the taste of that stew?' He got up and rummaged in a box. 'I picked up a Livarot at the local market. All right?'

'Perfect. I hope the English make good cheese. I'm not sure I can live without it.'

'We import it from France, so you won't have to go without.' He made room on the bread plate for the cheese and topped up her glass. 'I trust I'm not committing a dreadful social crime in French eyes by serving Livarot with burgundy?'

She smiled. 'The only crime was to serve that stew with the burgundy. It would be a guillotining offence if we were still in France.' She saw his raised eyebrow. 'I assure you, people have been guillotined for far less in my country.'

They relaxed as far as possible, given the narrow, hard chairs, and talked about the invention of the guillotine and divergent fates of the monarchy in England and France. Conversation roamed widely under the influence of the wine, and they found much common ground, despite their very different backgrounds. After the constant anxiety of the previous fortnight, Elisabeth could feel the tension slipping away.

'I must say, you have an impressive knowledge for one so young, Miss Duval.'

She helped herself to another slice of the cheese, which smelled divinely pungent. 'I'm eighteen. Not so much younger than you, I think.'

'Then I've had eight more years in the world than you. You must have studied at a good school.'

'Actually, I grew up on a farm and was taught by my parents. My mother was very well educated, as she was adopted by a wealthy family when her own mother died. She was taught to speak fluent English and German, and was surrounded by books on all manner of subjects. I'm envious. We had not so many books at home, although my mother was a great storyteller.'

'She did a fine job of teaching you English.'

'She made us all speak only English for two days every week, ever since I learned to talk. Many people she knew were forced to leave France for England, so she wished us to be prepared.'

'How did she come to live on a farm?'

'It's a long story, but the farm was a place of safety after her life during the years of revolution. And falling in love with my father had a lot to do with it. My father is brilliant in his own way. He had no education, but is curious about the world. When he isn't out in the garden or orchard, he's in the barn, building ... I don't remember the word in English ... but clever things, like a faster butter maker or a table with a hidden drawer. Leonardo Da Vinci was his hero.'

'Mine too. I have copies of his drawings of various inventions in our library at home.'

'I shall be pleased to see them. Da Vinci spent the last years of his life close to where I grew up. My father attempted to make his ... ah, I am losing my English words from the wine.' Elisabeth circled her finger in the air.

'His aerial screw invention? The flying machine?'

'Yes, just so. But it did not fly. Maybe one day.' All this talk of her parents made her feel homesick. She couldn't help but wonder how long it would be before she saw them again.

'You must miss them.'

She set down her glass and closed her eyes. 'Tell me about your family, Mr Godwin, if you will.'

'I have a brother called Frederick, who thinks a lot of himself, despite being only seventeen – or perhaps because he is only seventeen. And my sister, Anne, is twelve, as you know. She is a lovely child, intelligent and caring. I'm sure you will like her. Our father passed away a year and a half ago and our mother three months after him, so Anne only has her two brothers for company at the moment. I am always busy and often away, which means my sister is lonely.'

'Your brother lives at home?'

'Yes, but Frederick is not pleasant company for a young girl. He keeps trying to correct her, rather than encourage her. Fortunately, we have a wonderful housekeeper, Mrs Palmer, who is very fond of her. We had a governess, but she left some months ago. I suspect Anne's sharp wit and incessant stream of clever questions drove her to it. I would send Anne to school, but I haven't found one that would suit her.'

'Your situation must give you a lot of responsibility.'

'It certainly keeps me busy, now that my father is gone. The office is in a state of chaos most of the time. It's all I can do to make sure the right ship turns up at the right port and loads the agreed cargo. Fortunately, Mr Rivers is retiring from the sea life to take over the running of our office. The sea air plays havoc with his rheumatism these days, not that he'd ever admit it. This will be his last voyage.'

'A good man, I think.'

'He is. I am looking forward to working with him.' He gestured around at the piles of papers and ledgers. 'I only wish he could do the accounts as well. I can't keep up with it since our bookkeeper decided to retire and grow roses.'

Elisabeth pushed her chair back and rose to go. 'I thank you for a pleasant evening, Mr Godwin. I can see you have work to do, so I won't take more of your time.'

He rose too and bowed awkwardly. 'The pleasure was all mine.' He sighed deeply. 'It was nice to take a break and talk about something other than ships and bills. I do hope you choose to stay on with Anne.'

She paused at the door, hovering uncertainly. If she hadn't had the wine and he hadn't looked so forlorn amongst the piles of paper, she might never have mentioned it. But how could she not offer to help when he had been so kind to her? 'Mr Godwin, I would be pleased to assist with the accounts tomorrow, if you wish.'

He looked at her as if she was a madwoman. 'Is it normal for women to do such work in France?'

She shrugged. 'Perhaps not. But on a farm, there are always too many tasks, so each person has to help as they are best able. The Lord has seen fit to give me a talent for numbers, so I have been keeping accounts, and calculating the profit on peaches compared to apples, since I was Anne's age.'

He eyed her with renewed interest. 'Do tell me, which was the more profitable?'

'Peaches, most years, as they sell for a higher price for the same weight. But apples are more … robust – they do not go bad so fast – and any not sold can be made into cider. Actually, our cheese sells for the best price, but we only have two dairy cows, so we mostly keep it for ourselves. The same for the eggs and vegetables and pigs. With a little of everything, we never go hungry anymore.'

He was still shaking his head, whether in disbelief or in decline of her offer, she could not tell. 'I do not like to do nothing all day. It would be a favour to me if you would allow me to help.'

She left before he could muster a reply, but, after a solid night's sleep, she regained her memory for English words and reported for duty. Perhaps it was a sign of his desperation, but he was ready with a ledger and a large box of papers stuffed with hand-written bills. Unfortunately, he was called away before he could give precise instructions. It did not matter. A quick flick through the ledger was enough for her to work out their simple system of listing each item of cargo for each voyage against the purchase price. By the time he came back, with streaks of black down his face, she was halfway through the bills of lading for the current voyage.

He flicked the page over with a grubby finger, leaving a smear of tar on the page. 'Marvellous. Really marvellous. No problems then? Well, I'll get on with my work. Captain wants the caulking seen to and new gibs. Perhaps you can work out how we can make a profit out of this damnable business.'

The rest of the voyage passed uneventfully, bolstered by a sharp westerly wind. Elisabeth was relieved to find she did not suffer from seasickness, even when the wind rose and the waves swept over the increasingly opaque porthole. All she could see most of the time was a hazy coastline through a crust of salt. Gradually, the coast loomed larger, until she could make out the dazzlingly white cliffs of England's south-east coast, standing out in stark contrast to the iron-blue of the sea.

The last section of the journey was the slowest, beating a path against the prevailing wind into the mouth of the Thames River, where they engaged a steam tug to take them up the river to London. When the buildings became taller and more densely stacked together, she abandoned the tiny cabin with its limited view and took up a position at the rail, where she could feel the excitement first hand. Mr

Godwin wandered over from his spot by the helm to join her.

'I never imagined there could be so many ships in the world,' she said.

'It's the busiest waterway on earth. Wait until we get to the City of London – it's a grand sight no matter how many times you see it. The greatest city on earth.' He pointed over to the left. 'The Royal Observatory at Greenwich will be on our port side soon.'

He was called away again, leaving her to marvel alone at the sights. Elisabeth scanned the vast sprawl of buildings and endless acres of docks jammed with vessels of all shapes and sizes.

He reappeared again as they rounded a bend in the river and the horizon filled with an even more impressive landscape of tall buildings, towers and domes. 'The City of London,' he said, with pride, 'and our destination, London docks.'

Elisabeth gazed in awe at the massive stone edifice up-river from the dock. 'Is that the king's castle?'

'It's the Tower of London. You're more likely to meet prisoners and lions there than the king these days.'

'Lions? You are making a joke?'

'It's true. The Tower has long had a menagerie of wild animals. I believe they still have lions, tigers, bears, monkeys and serpents, but no longer an elephant. In the past, one could visit, but I've heard they may move the animals to Regent's Park.' The vessel bumped gently against the dock, setting off a flurry of activity. 'Welcome to London, Miss Duval. Come, our carriage awaits.'

'You do not wish to stay for the unloading?'

'Not today. They know what they're doing without me getting in their way. Besides, it's getting late, and I'd like to get home before dark.'

They took their leave of the captain, who waved them off distractedly, as he focussed on seeing the vessel properly moored and ready for unloading. Mr Rivers called out a cheery farewell from the aft deck, which she answered with a salute and a wave.

And then they were on dry land again. Oddly, the solid wharf felt as if it was moving under her feet. She stood swaying on the spot for several seconds, the only stationary figure amongst a seething mass of bodies and jostle of activity. Scores of muscled dockers hurried around like trails of giant ants, pushing overloaded carts and shouting in a dozen or more different languages, but rarely in any form of English that was recognisable to her ears. Uniformed officials darted amongst them, with sheaves of documents in their hands and frowns on their faces.

She clutched the canvas bag closely to her body as she raced after the rapidly disappearing form of Mr Godwin, who seemed entirely unperturbed by the mayhem and stench. She caught up with him near a line of carriages by the dock gates.

He reached out a hand to help her up into the carriage before realising his mistake. He turned the gesture into a vague wave and a hint of a wink. 'Up you get, lad, no time to waste.'

The Greatest City on Earth

The trip across London was so filled with enticing sights that Elisabeth kept her nose to the window the whole way. Her host seemed amused, rather than affronted, by this impoliteness. He kept up a stream of commentary about the buildings around them and their place in history – the Tower of London, the old Roman walls, the famous churches, the markets. He clearly loved this city to the roots of his soul.

They travelled through a maze of market lanes with charmingly appropriate names like Poultry, Bread Street and Honey Lane. She gasped as they entered a wide thoroughfare lined on both sides with a solid row of buildings, at least four or five storeys high, topped with brick chimneys belching smoke. So much smoke that the street seemed to be suspended under a thundercloud.

The street was bustling with carriages, carts and barrows, and every variety of person from top-hatted gentlemen to ragged urchins. A few ladies were strolling arm-in-arm with the gentlemen, in elaborate bonnets and colourful gowns, puffed at the sleeve and almost as wide at the skirt as they were tall. They strutted like peacocks amongst a crowd of dull peahens – the working women, in drab cotton dresses and simple caps, who were bowed down under their loads.

'Cheapside, the great thoroughfare of London,' he said. 'Fairly quiet at this time of the day, of course. You should see it in the morning. Over there is St Mary-le-Bow Church, built by Christopher Wren after the Great Fire. And up ahead you can see another of Wren's little churches.'

'St Paul's Cathedral! Oh my, it's even more impressive than I imagined,' she gushed, feeling like the naïve country girl she was. But truly, it was an amazing sight for anyone not used to grandeur on this scale, which was surely almost everybody. 'I promised my mother I would visit,' she explained.

'And so you shall. We live not far away.'

She sat back in her seat and attempted to regain a little decorum. Less than ten minutes later, the carriage drew up outside a three-storey brick townhouse set on a cobbled square with a pretty garden in the middle. The clamour of London's streets was muted here. Even the air seemed fresher, after the putrid mix of animal, vegetable and mineral odours that seemed to pervade the rest of London.

The front door to the house opened, and an impeccably dressed man came down the steps towards them. He was middle-aged, but held himself upright, giving the impression of both strength and dignity. Elisabeth wondered if this was Mr Godwin's father and, if so, how he would feel about having a bedraggled French farm girl staying in his house. Then she remembered that his father had passed away. An uncle, perhaps?

The man opened the carriage door and said, 'Good evening, Mr Godwin. I did not expect you back so soon.'

'Palmer. Good to see you. I've brought home a guest.'

Mr Godwin hopped out of the carriage and handed her down, forgetting that she was dressed as a boy. The driver raised his eyebrows, but said nothing as he took his fare and a tip that had him doffing his hat. No doubt he had seen many stranger sights in this city. Mr Palmer didn't even blink as he took both their bags and followed them up the steps.

'Our guest will be in the room next to Anne.'

That did make him blink. 'Certainly, sir.'

'And could you send Mrs Palmer to see me in the library, please?'

The butler, if that is what he was, disappeared into a room on the ground floor, while Elisabeth followed Mr Godwin up the stairs. The house had a warmth to it beyond the pleasant temperature. It had a homely feel, though it was grand by her standards and beautifully decorated with thick carpets, paintings, and carved balusters polished to a gleam. Well-lit compared to her home in France too, with oil lamps rather than candles.

The library took her breath away. She spotted the Da Vinci drawings on one wall, but her eyes were drawn back to the shelves of books. She drew breath again with a deep sigh. There were more books than she had ever seen before and a scattering of comfortable-looking armchairs to curl up in. She went over to the nearest shelves and scanned the spines. Natural history, nautical books, mathematics, philosophy. She felt like she was in a dream.

Mr Godwin was watching her with a wry grin. 'I'm pleased to see you weren't exaggerating about your enthusiasm for books.'

She suddenly realised she had not said a word since coming into the house. 'I apologise for my curiosity. What a magnificent collection you have. And a lovely house. I am truly grateful to be here.'

A soft tap on the door provided a welcome interruption. A slim, middle-aged lady with lamppost-straight posture entered the library.

'Ah, Mrs Palmer, my apologies for arriving so close to the dinner hour. No need to go to any extra effort – whatever you have in the larder will be fine.'

'Now, Mr Godwin, you know that'll not do at all. I had a feeling you'd be back, what with the strong winds we've been having, so I've a nice big roast on.'

'That sounds wonderful, especially after ship food. Might I ask you to take Miss Duval to the room next to Anne's and assist her to shed her disguise before dinner. She will be staying with us for at least the next few days, perhaps longer.'

Mrs Palmer's shrewd gaze took in her appearance without comment or obvious judgement. 'Will you come this way please, Miss Duval?' She led the way up another flight of stairs and opened the door to a delightful room decorated in cream and pale blue, with large windows overlooking the square below. The bed was enormous – almost as wide as the entire cabin on the ship – and was covered with a quilt that looked as soft as a cloud.

'Mr Godwin cannot have meant for me to be in this room. It is far too grand.'

'This is the room he specified, Miss Duval.' Mrs Palmer looked her straight in the eye. 'Mr Godwin is oftentimes too kind-hearted for his own good. I hope you will prove to be worthy of his trust.'

Elisabeth held her gaze without flinching. 'Your concern for Mr Godwin does you credit, Mrs Palmer. I assure you, I mean no harm. I paid for my passage to England to undertake a small task for a relative in need, nothing more. His kindness in offering me a place to stay for a few days will not be abused.'

Mrs Palmer continued to look into her eyes, until Elisabeth was on the brink of shrivelling under the intensity. Then, miraculously, she smiled. 'Well, that's fine then. How about I fetch you some nice hot water to wash in. Do you have a gown to wear to dinner?'

Elisabeth felt her face flush as she thought of how out of place in this house her much-worn Sunday dress would look. 'I won't be expected to dine with the family, will I? I have nothing suitable.'

Mrs Palmer looked her up and down again. 'Well now, you're such a wee thing, you'd probably fit into one of the dresses my daughter made when she was training to be a seamstress. She left them with me when she got married, for she was soon with child and no longer able to fit into them herself.' Mrs Palmer did not wait for a reply, but smiled and swept out of the room.

Elisabeth hardly knew what to do. She didn't want to touch anything in the room until her hands were scrubbed clean, so she took her best dress out of the canvas bag and hung it over a chair, where it drooped in limp wrinkles, mocking her. It had been pretty when new, the colour of a ripe plum, but had faded to a less attractive puce after repeated washes. Still good enough for Sunday best at the farm, but jarringly out of place in this grand home.

Fortunately, Mrs Palmer came back before she could lose her nerve and run back down the stairs and out into the darkening streets. The housekeeper put a large jug of steaming water on a corner wash-stand, made of white marble, next to a white cloth and the palest soap Elisabeth had ever seen. 'I'll look out a dress while you have a wash. Let me know if there is anything else you need, Miss Duval.'

This time, Elisabeth was able to get in a quick 'thank you' before the housekeeper left. As soon as the door closed, she stripped off the outer layer of boy's clothes, which were so stiff with salt, sweat and dirt that they almost stood up by themselves. With a sigh of relief, she unwound the bindings around her chest, which had been necessary to squash her curves into a less obviously feminine profile.

The water was sumptuously hot and absolute heaven after the limited facilities she had had access to since she left home. By the time she had finished, her skin was several shades lighter, while the water in the basin looked murkier than the Thames. Even better, she smelled of roses, instead of like something that had died in a grimy corner of a fish-market. She slipped on her best dress for want of any alternative.

She had brushed her hair and was pinning it up into some semblance of style in front of an ornate gilded mirror, when the housekeeper returned with a selection of gowns, accompanied by a young maid.

'My goodness, what a transformation, if I may say so. Maude here will help you dress. Try the dark blue one – it should look lovely with your blonde hair.'

'Thank you, Mrs Palmer, I really am most grateful.'

'I hope you will forgive my earlier rudeness. My husband and I are very fond of the family and perhaps a mite protective since their parents' deaths.'

'Entirely understandable, when faced with an unexpected foreigner who looks like a street urchin. I'm afraid I haven't had access to hot water, or a mirror, for over two weeks.'

Mrs Palmer gave a quick nod, which gave the impression of a test passed. 'Maude will take anything you wish to have washed, though I hazard a guess that the fireplace might be a better option for that lot.' She wrinkled up her nose as she gestured towards the pile of discarded clothes. 'Excuse me, I must attend to the dinner. Miss Anne and Mr Fredrick Godwin have arrived home. The whole family will be in the library when you are ready. Down the stairs, second door on the right.'

Luckily, Mrs Palmer's daughter was about the same height as Elisabeth and not as slim, so the dress could be altered to fit with a few well-placed stitches and a belt. Maude chattered on about fashions and hair-styles, but Elisabeth could only stare at the strange woman in the mirror, who looked nothing like her, apart from wearing her face. The gown was cut lower than her own dresses, making her feel exposed, but the soft fabric draped beautifully and flowed around her as she moved. Without a doubt, it was the loveliest dress she would ever be likely to wear.

Determined not to put off the moment any longer, she descended the stairs and stopped outside the library door, which was open wide enough for her to hear an angry male voice inside. She hovered uncertainly, neither wanting to interrupt nor to be found listening.

'Rivers came into the office to tell me you were back. He was under the impression you had offered him a job looking after the office, now that he's too decrepit to sail. He must be as crazy as he looks. I doubt he can even read!'

'Calm down, Frederick. Rivers is as sharp as a fish-hook and the very man we need to keep track of where all the ships are and what cargo they are carrying. Now that the business is growing again, it is too much for me to cope with by myself. He looks a bit rough, perhaps, but a haircut and a decent suit will fix that.'

'Really, John, you should pension the old codger off. You're too soft.' There was a pause, accompanying by a clink of glassware. 'Talking of which, Rivers also said you've taken in a French runaway. If the boy runs off with all our silver, don't say I didn't warn you.'

Elisabeth rather felt that was her cue to enter. Three cross faces turned to her as she knocked lightly and entered.

John Godwin choked on his drink, but recovered his poise after a brief fit of coughing. He rose from the armchair next to Anne and smiled. 'Ah, there you are. May I introduce Miss Duval, who has come over from France and will be staying with us for a while.'

The stout figure of Frederick Godwin stood by the sherry decanter, with a full glass in his hand, staring at her with an open mouth. His face was round and red-cheeked – but petulant, rather than jolly – quite the opposite of his brother's slim, sun-browned face. 'Rivers said you brought back a boy.'

John Godwin grinned at him. 'How on earth could this enchanting young lady ever be mistaken for a boy? You must have misheard him, Frederick.'

Frederick blushed to the roots of his hair. 'Then might I ask who she is and what the devil is she doing here?' he blurted, before remembering his manners and sketching a cursory bow in her direction.

His older brother's grin grew a little wider. 'I very much hope Miss Duval will be our new bookkeeper.'

'Really, John, how much of a fool do you take me for? How preposterous.' Frederick tossed down the sherry in a single gulp and stalked out of the room, banging the door behind him.

Anne rose from the settee and took Elisabeth's hand. 'Forgive my brother's appalling manners, Miss Duval. You are very welcome. As you can see, I am in great need of sensible female company, having only two older brothers who tease and quarrel all the time like a couple of tomcats. Come and sit by me and tell me all about yourself. John, do stop smirking and get Miss Duval a sherry.'

Elisabeth smothered a smile and took a seat beside her. Anne seemed to have the measure of her brothers, despite only being twelve. She was tall for her age – almost the same height as Elisabeth – and very like her older brother, both to look at and, apparently, in temperament. Her soft brown eyes were alight with curiosity and humour, although set in a serious face, with the same slim, angular planes as John Godwin.

The latter passed her an ornate crystal glass filled with sherry and sat down in the armchair at right-angles to the settee, without saying a word or taking his eyes off her. She wondered if she had made some faux pas in dressing, but possibly he was simply finding her current state difficult to reconcile with the boy he had come to know aboard the ship. If so, he would not be the only one, for she herself felt like a cuckoo in a robin's nest.

Anne's gaze flicked between them, giving Elisabeth the impression that she was not a girl who missed much.

'How did you come to meet my brother, Miss Duval?'

'He was recommended to us at the port of Le Havre in France, when I was in need of transport to England.'

'But John never takes passengers.'

Both of them turned to look at him, but he simply shrugged and said, 'I do occasionally.'

Anne raised her eyebrows, as if this was news to her.

'What? You think I should have left her to take her chances on the docks?'

'Of course not, John. But, my goodness, she must have turned some heads on board.'

'I doubt they could have looked away long enough to trim the sails, if she had travelled as she is now.'

Now it was Elisabeth's turn to feel uncomfortable, although less so since Frederick had left the room. 'Your brother is teasing me, Miss Godwin. I was dressed as a boy to avoid unwanted attention, having ridden by horse from the Loire Valley, some distance to the south.'

'How brave of you. You must have been desperate to come all this way.'

'I promised to carry a package to England for a relative. Your brother has been kind enough to invite me to stay in your home for a few days, for which I am very grateful.'

'And now you have no need of a disguise any longer.'

'On the contrary, I am still very much in disguise. My own clothes are only fit to be worn on a farm. This dress was made by Mrs Palmer's daughter, who is clearly an excellent seamstress.'

'You do look lovely, Miss Duval. Doesn't she, John?'

He was saved from answering by the dinner bell.

'Are you really going to work as a bookkeeper?' Anne asked as they entered the dining room.

'If she wants the job,' John replied, at the same instant as Elisabeth said, 'That was said in jest.'

John Godwin pulled out the chair to the right of the head of the table for Elisabeth. 'Miss Duval was kind enough to assist with the accounts while we were crossing from France. She was very quick and managed to detect some errors that would have cost the business dearly.'

Anne took the seat opposite Elisabeth and examined her with the intensity of a dedicated naturalist inspecting a strange new breed of butterfly. 'Are women allowed to do anything in France? Can they be a bookkeeper? Or a doctor?'

At that moment, Mr Palmer appeared with a tureen. He served up a broth thick with vegetables, which smelled heavenly. When the soup was served, Elisabeth looked to Mr Godwin, not wanting to encourage Anne's ambitions too overtly if it was against the family's wishes.

'I would be interested to hear too,' he said.

'Well, then, I expect France is no different from England. People tell you what you cannot do, for no reason other than being a woman or poor or some other imagined deficit. I feel it's best to ignore them and get on with life, in whatever way you can. There are woman nurses and healers better than many doctors, although it is true that they cannot undertake formal medical training. As for me, no one else in my family likes to keep the accounts, so the task fell to me.'

'Perhaps the more women who chose their own path, the more society will come to accept it?'

'Perhaps, Mr Godwin, but I fear such change will be slow to come, if left to the whims of society. In the meantime, surely no harm can come from reading a book or two on medicine, don't you think, Miss Godwin?'

'I do,' said Anne firmly. 'I wish you would call me Anne. Miss Godwin sounds so formal. Is that all right, John?'

John Godwin held up his hands in surrender. 'An hour in the house and Miss Duval already has us turning conventions upside down.'

Elisabeth felt the colour rise in her cheeks. 'I must apologise for being so forward. I grew up in a household where debate was valued over good manners.'

'I did not mean it as a criticism, Miss Duval. In fact, I was about to say what a refreshing change it makes. You are part of our household now, so Anne and John it is.'

'Then I am Elisabeth. In truth, my name is Elisabeth Duchamp, not Duval, but I would prefer to keep to the latter for the present, if that is acceptable. I will tell you the full story if you wish, since I am to be honoured with your trust.'

'I would be pleased to hear it.' He turned to Anne, whose grin stretched from ear to ear. 'Shall we go on an expedition tomorrow to find a medical text suitable for a twelve-year-old girl, if such a thing exists? But this is a compromise, Anne. You must keep up your other studies as well, especially your music.'

'Of course,' Anne said, clapping her hands gleefully.

The soup course was cleared, while Anne launched into a stream of questions about Elisabeth's opinion of London, her preferences in literature, her favourite things, and her life in France. The joint of beef was being carved, and laughter filled the air, when Frederick appeared and took the seat at the far end of the table.

'Frederick, you'll never guess where Elisabeth is taking me tomorrow,' Anne said. 'We're going to visit a bookshop, then take a picnic luncheon to the park, and John is to come too.'

'Eating out of doors, where everyone can see you? What on earth are you thinking?' Frederick helped himself to a glass of wine. 'John, don't you have work to do?'

'I do, but I can spare an hour in the middle of the day to eat. Do join us, Frederick. It will be fun.'

'Fun?' He cut into the beef with gusto, spearing a Yorkshire pudding to go with it, and slathering both in gravy. 'Anyway, it cannot be tomorrow. I am dining at my club. John, I do wish you would come with me. Farley-Hampton is sure to be there, and it's high time the matter was settled.'

'Frederick, I have told you time and again, just like I told our father, that I do not wish to marry the Hampton girl, no matter how well connected and wealthy her father is. She's as dull as ship's food and twice as likely to give me indigestion. And her parents aren't much better.'

'Don't be a fool, John. She's pretty and amenable – what more do you need? It would be a fine match, and you know the business would profit from the alliance when we need it most.'

'Marry her yourself, if that's all you want in a wife. There are other ways of improving the profit from the business, as long as we can sort our peaches from our apples.'

'Have you gone quite mad?'

The two brothers glared at each other across the expanse of white linen, while Anne rolled her eyes at Elisabeth, who directed her eyes down and concentrated on enjoying the meal.

When her meal was finished and the silence had stretched beyond the bearable, Elisabeth turned to Frederick and said, 'We can have the picnic another day, if you would care to join us.'

'Can we still go to the bookshop?' Anne pleaded.

Elisabeth could see that John's thoughts were far away, so she gathered up her napkin. 'A lovely dinner, thank you. Mrs Palmer is a splendid cook. Anne, would you care to join me in the library and show me your favourite books?'

Anne pushed her chair back and raced for the door. Elisabeth followed more sedately, so she overheard John agreeing to go with Frederick to see Mr Farley-Hampton. Perhaps the needs of the shipping business would have to take precedence, after all. Such was the way of the world.

Anne's favourite books were in her room, so it was more than an hour before Elisabeth returned to the library. After the excitements of the day, she was ready to drop with exhaustion into the divinely soft bed in her room, but she felt it would be impolite not to wish her host goodnight first.

At first, she thought the library was empty. A single lamp lit the area around the armchairs and settee, throwing the rest of the room into semi-darkness. She had turned to leave when John Godwin rose from a seat in the alcove by the window.

'Will you stay a moment, Miss Duval? ... Elisabeth.'

She sat on the settee, waiting for him to continue.

He moved to a spot by the fire, which had burned down to a soft glow. 'Seeing Anne come alive this evening has made me realise how much she has been in need of lively female company.'

'And this is why you have decided to marry Miss Farley-Hampton?'

'What? No! I have no intention of marrying her and it is high time her father is told so clearly and unequivocally. I have procrastinated far too long.' He came over and sat in the armchair. 'I am aware you have your reasons for travelling to England. Perhaps it would be best if I know what your intentions are, before Anne becomes too fond of you. Although, I rather suspect it may already be too late in that regard.'

'May I tell you the whole story? I would value your advice.'

'By all means.'

They were interrupted by a knock on the door and the welcome sight of Mrs Palmer with a tray of coffee. Elisabeth was glad of a moment to get her thoughts together and took the opportunity to thank Mrs Palmer for the delicious dinner, to her evident surprise and pleasure.

When they were alone again, Elisabeth began from the start. 'I think I mentioned that my mother was adopted into a wealthy family. They suffered great loss during the years of revolution, but my mother felt a strong loyalty to the family and was able to help by hiding some valuables. My mother's adoptive sister, my aunt, returned from exile for a few years, only to be forced to leave France again several weeks ago, when the king abdicated and a new usurper seized power. My aunt knew she would never be allowed to leave with anything valuable, so she did us the honour of asking for our assistance again.'

John put his cup down and began drumming his fingers on the arm of the chair. 'She expected an eighteen-year-old woman to travel all the way to England with these valuables? Why did your father not go?'

'I was a late blessing to their marriage. My parents are too old now to make such an arduous journey. My aunt thought my brother would go, but he has a family and a farm to look after, so I offered. In truth, the decision was forced upon us, as soldiers were sent to our farm to retrieve the items by force.'

He stopped drumming and looked up with a start. 'What happened?'

'We escaped, although my mother was injured. I left my parents in hiding and rode as fast as I could to my brother's house. As you know, my brother travelled with me as far as Le Havre.'

'Well, that explains your need to travel in disguise. Whatever you are carrying must be extremely valuable for them to go to so much trouble.'

'It is an exquisite pearl necklace in a jewellery box made by the most famous designer in France. Both items are of enormous value, but their true worth is in what they mean to the family. My mother told me the necklace is always handed down by the head of the family to his wife. That is rightfully my aunt, but there is a distant cousin who feels his claim is greater. He is determined to have the necklace and has the power and wealth to insist upon it by any means possible.'

'As evidenced by the soldiers. I would like to hear the story of your escape sometime, but it might be better to focus on what you wish to do now that you are safe in London.'

'For which I have you to thank.'

'That you made it this far is much more to do with your own courage. You are an extraordinary young woman, Elisabeth.'

She shook her head. 'No. Only an ordinary woman in an extraordinary situation.' She set her coffee cup down on the tray. 'You asked my intentions. First, I must make contact with a bookseller, who passes messages for French exiles in need. Then I must wait for a reply, however long that takes. My mother suggested it would be safer for me to stay away from France for several weeks at least, or until she sends a message. But I would prefer to return home as soon as possible to make sure my family is safe.'

He leaned back and started drumming his fingers again. After a few seconds' thought, he evidently came to a decision. 'You must stay here until we are certain it is safe for you to return.' He held up a hand before she could dissent. 'I can send one of my men to check on your parents.'

She sat back again, seeing that this was a more sensible plan.

'The bookseller is in London, I take it?'

'Yes, he is. Would you close your eyes for a moment, please?' When he did so, she slipped her fingers down into the hidden pocket of her corset and withdrew the slip of paper. 'Here is the address.'

He smoothed it out, with a slight smile. 'Mr Arthur Postlethwaite. This address is only about a mile away, near the British Museum. Another place you must visit during your stay.'

'I will go to his shop tomorrow and purchase a book on medicine for Anne while I am there.'

'We will all go. It is unsafe for a woman to be out on her own in this city. And now, I think it is past time for you to get some sleep. It has been a long day.'

Elisabeth was more than happy to comply. As she slipped between the smooth sheets, she gave thanks for finding a guardian angel with good sense as well as kindness, before dropping into a deep sleep.

The next morning, she was awakened by an insistent knocking at the door. In her drowsy state, she thought it must be her mother, waking her to milk the cows, until she recalled where she was. Sun was filtering through the soot-laden air, which meant it was already high enough in the sky to shine over the surrounding buildings.

Anne poked her head around the door. 'Elisabeth, you're awake at last. Come and have breakfast, then we can go to buy my book.'

The head disappeared again before Elisabeth could reply. She pushed herself out from under the covers reluctantly, before realising she had nothing suitable to wear. She was pondering whether last night's evening gown or her own Sunday best would be the lesser evil, when Maude appeared with hot water and, after a discreet interval, Mrs Palmer arrived with a selection of day clothes and hats.

Mrs Palmer laid out the dresses on the bed and ran a professional eye over her charge. With a nod, she picked out a dress of a deep coppery hue, like autumn leaves. Elisabeth would never have chosen it herself, but when it was on and pinned to size, she acknowledged that Mrs Palmer had excellent taste. Thankfully, the sleeves were long and the neckline modestly high, although the waist was nipped in tightly above the full skirt. She chose a bonnet to go with it, with a brim wide enough to hide much of her face, and a shawl to keep her warm.

Anne was waiting for her in the dining room, eager to discuss the plan for the day ahead. 'Have a peach, Elisabeth. John sent out specially to get them fresh from the market this morning.'

'I will, they look delicious,' Elisabeth replied, and that was the last word she got into the flow until she had taken her last sip of tea. 'Your ideas sound lovely, Anne, but perhaps we do not have to see all the sights of London on the first day. I was hoping to rest a little in the afternoon and listen to you play the piano.'

'All right, if that is what you would prefer. Are you finished? Shall I get John? He said to as soon as you are ready.'

Anne bounded off and reappeared soon after with her brother in tow, looking far more like a city gentleman than he had on board the ship. He slipped on a long black morning coat over his dark green waistcoat, adjusted his cravat, and added a tall silk hat. 'Everybody ready? Anne, where is your shawl?'

While Anne raced away to get it, he turned to Elisabeth. 'Good morning, Elisabeth. May I say that colour suits you well? Shall I call for a carriage or would you prefer to walk?'

'A walk would be wonderful, if it's only a mile.' After days of forced inactivity aboard the ship, preceded by days of muscle-pounding riding, she was looking forward to stretching her legs.

At almost ten o'clock in the morning, the streets were chaotic with people and carriages, even more than there had been the previous evening. Although it was fascinating to observe the astonishing diversity of life in London, Elisabeth did feel rather overwhelmed by the crowds and appalled at the stink of raw sewage in the streets. The number of children also surprised her, many of them wearing clothes little better than rags, hawking a few items at the side of the road or wandering aimlessly.

John must have noticed her puzzlement. 'Poverty is a serious problem in London. Children of families who cannot afford schooling must find a way to make what money they can. Many children work in factories or sweeping chimneys, and others do what they can on the streets. You must watch out for the pickpockets, or they'll have your purse before you even know they're there.'

She was about to ask how to spot a pickpocket when she was knocked sideways by a small boy with a dripping nose and filthy clothes. John picked him up by the collar, checked his pockets, and sent him on his way, clutching a bright copper coin. He tucked her arm through his and guided her through the crowd, keeping Anne close on his other side.

They reached the premises of Mr Postlethwaite without further incident. The frontage on the street was narrow, but she could see, through the small panes of glass in the half-round windows, that the packed shelves of books ran deep into the building behind. Elisabeth kept her head down as they pushed open the ancient door, setting off a bell that summoned the proprietor. He was a man of some threescore years, so short that he was barely visible over the top of the counter, with wisps of white hair and piercingly intelligent eyes.

'Good morning, sir, madam. And a fine morning it is. How may I be of assistance today?'

They had agreed that John would do the talking until they were certain of the man they were dealing with. 'Good morning. Would you be Mr Arthur Postlethwaite?'

'Indeed, I am, sir. Proprietor of this fine establishment these past four decades, at your service.'

'We wish to purchase a book on medicine for a young person who is considering becoming a doctor.'

'Very good, sir. I would recommend Mr William Burdon's *Domestic Medicine: A Treatise on the Prevention and Cure of Diseases*. An excellent introduction to diseases of all types. As it happens, I have recently acquired a copy in excellent condition from a young man who discovered that medicine was no longer his métier. An unexpected aversion to blood, as I recall.' He scuttled off into the shadows of the shelves, where the sounds of a ladder being slid across the floor mingled with a series of puffs and grunts.

John cast a glance through the window to the street outside. He moved beside Elisabeth and whispered in her ear, 'The man across the street appears to be watching this shop. He has the bearing of a soldier and the style of a Frenchman. I noticed him as we came in and he has not moved for five minutes at least. I suggest you do not look up.'

A shiver ran up her spine, but she resisted the urge to look. 'Can you see if he has a cut down the side of his face, from his eye to his mouth.'

'I think not. Shall we leave?'

'I expect we are safe enough, as there is nothing to suggest we are anything more than a normal harmless English family out to buy a book. I would hate to disappoint Anne.'

Mr Postlethwaite reappeared, holding a book bound in rich brown morocco. 'On the topmost shelf, naturally.'

'Anne, would you care to have a look?'

If the proprietor was startled to see a young girl come forward and leaf through the book, he made no comment. Anne nodded enthusiastically, so John paid for the book and handed it back to her when it was wrapped.

'I wish you well with your studies, young lady,' the bookseller said. 'Come back when you are ready to move on to advanced anatomy. Now, is there something else I can help you with, sir?'

Elisabeth turned to face to the counter, feeling emboldened by having John close behind her. '*Bonjour*, Monsieur Postlethwaite. I have been given your name by a friend, who was to leave a message for me here.'

The bookseller turned narrowed eyes in her direction. 'Your name, madame?'

'Mademoiselle Elisabeth Duchamp. The message may be in the name of my brother, Henri Duchamp.'

He continued to examine her for several seconds, with only a flaring of his nostrils showing a spark of interest and recognition of the name. 'You should have come alone.'

'I trust this man with my life and so can you.'

'Hmph, so you say.' He let further seconds pass. 'Very well. I have a message. A reply is expected.'

The bell tinkled again as the door opened. Elisabeth felt John turn his head slightly, then his arm went around her shoulder and his fingers pressed lightly into her upper arm.

'My dear, look at the time. We must hurry or we'll be late for our engagement with our dear friends, the Hamptons. Good day to you, Mr Postlethwaite.'

John's arm pulled her closer to his side. Elisabeth could see a bead of sweat form on the bookseller's forehead.

'Wait, sir. Do not forget your collection of romantic poetry.' He pushed a slim volume across the counter. 'I'm sure your wife will particularly enjoy Lord Byron's work.'

John scooped up the book and slipped it into an inner pocket. 'Thank you, sir. I must have forgotten all about it in my haste.'

They turned to go out. Elisabeth, with her gaze fixed on the floor and her face concealed by the wide brim of her bonnet, could see only the man's highly polished boots, standing directly in the middle of the path to the door. Anne was on the other side of the man, inching away and clutching her parcel. Suddenly, she tripped over a stack of books, sending it tumbling across the man's feet. The boots jumped to avoid the cascade, with Anne's flailing arms adding to the confusion, allowing John and Elisabeth to slip past on the other side.

'I beg your pardon, sir, I wasn't watching where I was going,' Anne said, as she scrambled upright and walked calmly out the door.

They strolled at a normal pace down the street, with John's arm firmly holding Elisabeth back from her instinct to run. Anne skipped along beside them until they turned the next corner.

John leaned down and whispered, 'Definitely no scar.'

'Not the soldier who attacked my family, then. That's a relief.'

'What's going on?' Anne interrupted. 'Who was that man and why were you frightened of him, Elisabeth?'

'Probably simply a loiterer with no manners looking for a book,' John said, 'but there are plenty of dangerous thieves in London, so it's always wise to be cautious.' He took in Anne's dubious expression and added, 'What a happy coincidence that you knocked the pile of books into him, despite the improbable angle. And how lucky that you managed to hold on to your own book, despite falling over in such a dramatic fashion.'

The ends of Anne's lips twitched up into an impish grin before she continued skipping, her book clutched against her chest.

Back at the house, John suggested Anne go to her room to read her new acquisition. She turned her gaze on each of them for long enough to show that she was fully aware they were deliberately excluding her, then raced up the stairs. John ushered Elisabeth into the library and rang for tea.

'Sometimes I think my sister is too smart for her own good.'

Elisabeth slumped down into an armchair and yanked off her bonnet, setting her carefully restrained hair loose. 'I cannot allow you and Anne to be put in danger again. I will leave this afternoon.'

He sat down next to her and leaned in, his voice a fierce whisper. 'Absolutely not. How do you think I would feel, knowing you were out there, unprotected, with men like that after you? I would rather cut off my right arm than send you out unprotected.'

Elisabeth felt the hairs on the back of her neck stand up. She turned to the door and saw Frederick standing there.

'Time to go, John, or we'll miss Farley-Hampton.'

'Sorry, Frederick, it'll have to be another day. Urgent business to attend to.'

Frederick looked between them and sneered, 'I can guess what that might be. You're a fool, John. If you don't marry the Hampton girl, our father's debts will sink us all.' The door banged behind him.

Elisabeth suddenly realised how it might look to Frederick. Her with a flushed face and loose hair, John leaning in so intently, and Frederick so obviously predisposed to think the worst of her. She tried to stutter out an apology as she scooped up her hair and fixed it in place, but John was so incensed that he wasn't listening. He strode towards the door wearing an expression that would have made a regiment of soldiers cower, slamming the door behind him with enough force to rattle the glassware.

She curled up in the armchair, uncertain whether to be steadfast or retreat to her room. A soft tap signalled the arrival of Mrs Palmer with a tray of tea and cake, which she deposited on the table, before hastening for the door without comment. Elisabeth could hear John's voice outside, so she bent over to pour the tea to cover her discomfort, as he came back into the room and flopped into the chair beside her.

John took the proffered cup, closing his eyes as he sipped the tea and regained his composure. Slowly, the flush on his cheeks dulled, but the stress lines on his brow remained, making him look years older. 'That was utterly unforgivable. I'm so sorry, Elisabeth. I wish my brother would have a little more faith in my ability to make the business a success, without sacrificing my happiness to the Hamptons.'

She wanted to reach out and comfort him, but she kept her hands firmly on the bone china cup. 'He should sail with you, as I did, so he understands how hard you work and how respected you are by all those who deal with you. I could see it in the crew's attitude and with the innkeeper, who told us you were the only one he would trust. That kind of trust breeds success.'

He looked down and, for a moment, seemed about to unburden himself, but all he said was, 'Thank you.'

'John, you are the kindest man I have ever met, but I cannot in good conscience take advantage of it any further. It is plainly obvious that I am causing a disruption in your family. I really must go.'

'No. I won't let you. You must learn to ignore Frederick. He has long felt that I am an overbearing older brother, while I think he is a pompous idiot. Unfortunately, we're both right.' He pulled the slim book out of his pocket and attempted a weak smile. 'Anyway, you cannot go until you've read the poetry book.'

She'd forgotten all about it in the rush to get away from the bookshop.

John flipped through the pages until he came to one marked by a sealed note. '*She Walks in Beauty*, by Lord Byron'.

'She walks in beauty, like the night
Of cloudless climes and starry skies;
And all that's best of dark and bright
Meet in her aspect and her eyes;
Thus mellowed to that tender light
Which heaven to gaudy day denies.'

He handed the note to her, unopened.

She read it and handed it back to him. 'My aunt suggests I name a time and place to meet in London. Her situation is precarious – she is being watched. She may have to leave England again soon.'

'Then we must come up with a plan to ensure both your safety and hers.'

'I have to admit it is a great relief for me to have your friendship and support. I cannot imagine how I would have coped with all this on my own in an unknown city.'

'I'm pleased to help. Meanwhile, I insist you stay here and not leave this house without me. Unfortunately, I really must get back to work, but I'll do as much as I can from home.'

'I'll write back to my aunt as soon as possible.'

'Palmer can take the message. He's completely trustworthy and so unequivocally English that he is unlikely to be suspected by anyone watching the shop.'

Keeping the Promise

Ten days later, John and Elisabeth took a carriage to Hyde Park. They travelled along Oxford Street, one of the grand streets of London, but it might as well have been a country lane, for all the notice Elisabeth took. Instead, her mind was churning behind closed eyelids, alternating between thoughts of what lay ahead and the comforting warmth of the man beside her.

She fingered the cameo brooch her aunt had given her, which she was hoping would act as a good luck charm. If her aunt came in person – which seemed unlikely – then at least she would know Elisabeth from the brooch. Elisabeth hadn't seen her since she was a child and couldn't recall what she looked like.

The plan was simple enough. They were to leave the carriage on West Carriage Drive, near the bridge, and walk through the south-west corner of Hyde Park to the path beside the Serpentine. The tall trees that graced the park were fairly widely spaced at that point, allowing a degree of privacy, a view in all directions, and a quick escape route, should the encounter go wrong.

John had been reluctant to let her make the delivery herself, but she had insisted. She had promised her mother that she would undertake this task, and that was a promise she intended to keep, no matter what. She had compromised with John to the extent of allowing him to carry the jewellery box until they were certain it could be handed over safely. Now, as the carriage came to a halt between the leafy beauty of Kensington Gardens on one side and Hyde Park on the other, John adjusted the bag hanging around his neck, pulled his overcoat around it and turned to her, with one eyebrow raised. She looked into his eyes and nodded.

They had arrived early, so they strolled beside the murky green water of the Serpentine, under a red and gold umbrella of leaves beginning their autumn transformation. John's quiet stream of conversation calmed her nerves enough to enjoy the beauty of the park.

'I have happy memories of Hyde Park. We used to come here for grand celebrations when I was a child. This is the first place I saw fireworks and a giant hot-air balloon. I recall a magnificent event when I was about ten years old, when they re-enacted the Battle of Trafalgar on the Serpentine. The band played the anthem, and the crowd cheered when the French fleet sank in the lake.' John smiled as he saw it in his mind, then gave her a rueful glance. 'My apologies. That was not very tactful of me. Perhaps we should talk of William the

Conqueror instead? Did you know he built the Tower of London?'

'Ah, the English and the French. We are always divided, even when we are close.'

'As nations, perhaps. It does not mean our peoples cannot be friends.'

'No indeed.'

Few people were about so early. An arthritic old man hobbled slowly along in front of them, supported by a thick cane, and wearing a coat that looked four sizes too large. He reminded her a little of Mr Rivers, or rather, what Mr Rivers might be like in ten years if fate was unkind. Not far away, a burly gardener, with rolled shirtsleeves and a moss-green waistcoat, raked the leaves to and fro, to little effect.

Elisabeth took a second glance, thinking his profile seemed vaguely familiar. The gardener tipped his cap and continued raking. Mr Palmer. Her eyes shifted back to the bent figure of the old man. It was Mr Rivers, looking almost unrecognisable in his newly clean-shaven and disguised state. She caught John's eye and raised her eyebrows, but he just smiled that enigmatic Godwin smile she had seen so often on both brother and sister.

Up ahead, a woman in a black dress and veiled hat strolled towards them from the opposite direction, walking with regal grace beside a tall man of military bearing. She sat down on a park bench, a little stiffly, but with a straight back and head held proudly high. He stood with feet apart, several yards away, looking every inch the soldier on watch.

Elisabeth's pulse did a little dance. 'Could it be that my aunt has come herself, rather than send a messenger?'

Mr Rivers stopped by the lake, throwing a few crusts of bread to an eager cluster of squabbling ducks. They walked on past him to the bench, where John squeezed her arm gently before releasing it. When she was seated beside the woman, he withdrew a few yards, with his back to the Serpentine and his eyes scanning the few early strollers. The gardener slowly raked his way in their direction.

Two elegantly dressed men were strolling towards them, deep in conversation and taking no notice of their party. They took a seat by the lake, too far away to overhear. Without so much as a glance in their direction, one of the men opened a copy of *The Times* and their faces disappeared from view.

The woman beside Elisabeth lifted her veil, revealing a face not unlike her own mother's face, although far more drawn with sorrow. She kissed Elisabeth's cheeks with lips as dry as the fallen leaves around her feet. When she spoke, her voice was so quiet and husky that Elisabeth had to strain to catch her words. Hearing French spoken again after so many weeks gave her an odd sensation of sliding back in time.

'My dearest niece, how wonderful to see you again after so many years. How grown up and elegant you are.' She reached out thin fingers to the brooch. 'It gives me great pleasure to see you wearing this, although I would have known you even without the brooch. You are the very image of your dear mother.' She lifted the lacy edge of her cloak to reveal an almost identical cameo.

'I did not expect to see you, Aunt,' Elisabeth replied, slipping easily back into her native language, 'although I am delighted that you came. I wish I could have seen more of you, knowing how close you were to my mother.'

Her aunt sighed and grasped Elisabeth's hands. 'I would have liked to know you better too. If only it had been possible.'

'I remember you visiting once when I was a little girl. I still have the beautiful quilt you gave me. I used to lie awake at night tracing the embroidered trees and birds with my fingers. It gave me courage in the darkness.'

'We all need a little of that, my dear.' Her aunt wiped away a tear with a dainty black glove. 'I did not expect you to come either. I do hope nothing untoward has happened to your brother?'

'Henri has a family now and a farm to run. We thought it best if I came instead.'

'I was desperately worried for you all. It was a moment of madness on my part to risk your family's safety by sending your mother the jewellery box. I have regretted it every minute of every day since. When my messenger was forced to reveal its location, I feared I had signed your death warrant.' Her aunt examined Elisabeth's attempt at a blank expression. 'Pray tell me what really happened.'

'Soldiers came, but we were all able to escape. My parents went into hiding and I rode off with the jewellery box.'

'Oh, my dear, I am so sorry. I was fearful he would send that fiend, Victor Cloutier. You would not wish to meet him – a huge, vicious beast, who has been responsible for many terrible deeds and brutal deaths.'

'Their leader was such a man.'

Her aunt shuddered and gripped her hands more tightly. 'Then you did well to escape. Did anyone suffer injury?'

'Cloutier was knocked out. He will have a nasty scar to warn people of his evil nature.'

'Your parents?'

Elisabeth hesitated, but decided not to add to her aunt's worries by mentioning her mother's wound. 'They were well when I left them. As much in love as ever and probably having a fine time toasting each other with wine in the cheese cave.'

Her aunt's smile lit up her face. 'I envy your mother and father that happiness. Not that they didn't deserve it and more. Did she talk much about the past?'

'Not at all. I know only terrible things happened, but my mother refused to talk about it. I wanted to know more, but I did not wish to upset her.'

'Your mother is the bravest and most selfless person I have ever known. Did you know she risked her own life to save mine? You should be very proud of her. And your father too, who risked his life for both of us, and made my darling sister happy again. But your mother is absolutely right – we must look to the future and not dwell on the horrors of the past.'

'You knew my father? I thought they met later.'

'Your father was the nephew of a gardener on our estate when we were all young. I understand he had to leave his family farm to earn a living, as harvests had been poor and times were difficult. Not that I knew that at the time. Titled families lived in comfort, ignorant of the people's suffering, to our shame. I was so grateful to be given the chance to help him get his family farm back.'

'What were they like when they were young?'

'Your parents were the best of friends, right from the start, and always great fun. Your father had a wonderful way with animals. He was given the job of leading all the younger children around on the pony. At the end of the ride, he would climb up a tree like a little monkey and throw apples down to us. Your mother couldn't stand to be left out, so she went up too, when the governess wasn't looking. I was not allowed to, of course, as it was not fitting behaviour for a young lady, nor possible in the ridiculous gowns I had to wear.'

Elisabeth smiled to think of them, so like François and herself. 'She was very grateful to your family for taking her in and giving her an education and a home.'

'How she loved to learn. I admit I took advantage of it by making her learn how to copy my handwriting, so she could do the lessons our tutor set for us. We did everything together, except that she did not have to attend formal events or learn court etiquette, which seemed to me to take up much of my day. We even looked alike, enough so that many of the servants could be fooled. As you can imagine, we used that to full advantage.'

Her aunt had a faraway look in her eyes and a smile on her lips. It gave Elisabeth great comfort to know that their lives had been so happy before the revolution tore their world apart. She lowered her voice to a whisper. 'She was honoured that you asked her to look after the jewellery box, as it obviously means a lot to you both. I have it here to give to you.'

Her aunt seemed not to have heard her. She loosened her grip on Elisabeth's hands a little and stared off into the distance. 'I will have to leave England again soon. Not for France, of course. I hold little hope of ever seeing my homeland again. Oh Elisabeth, I am tired of this life and wish only to retire in peace somewhere safe, as far from my treacherous cousin as possible.'

'I will pray that you achieve that peace, as you deserve.'

'I was hoping I might persuade you to come with me. Your mother regrets that you have not had the opportunities of education and travel, which I would be delighted to offer you. I have corresponded with her on the matter and she says the decision must be up to you alone. My reasons are entirely selfish, I admit, as I wish to enjoy more of your company. You remind me so much of our younger selves.'

Elisabeth glanced over to where John was standing. His eyes stopped their relentless scan of the park and turned to her, as if he had sensed her gaze. Her heart fluttered as his eyes met hers.

Her aunt watched the exchange with interest. 'I see. I trust he is a good man?'

'The best.'

'Then I wish you every happiness. Elisabeth, I would like you to keep the pearl necklace and the jewellery box. I fear they will never rest safely in my hands, no matter where I am. Your family certainly deserves them more than *he* does.' Her aunt spat out the word 'he' with venom, before dropping her voice to a low murmur. 'It would make me happy to think of you wearing the necklace, although I would advise you to do so discreetly, only in trusted company. Guard the jewellery box closely too, for it is even more precious.'

'You misunderstand me, aunt. Mr Godwin is a dear friend, but no more. And it would not be right for me to keep something so valuable, as we are not related by blood.' She caught John's eye again and waved him over. As John moved towards them, he unbuttoned his coat and slipped the strap of the bag over his head.

'Elisabeth, I insist. Family is about strength of love and loyalty, not the weaker link of blood. I think of your mother as my true sister, which makes you the future matriarch of this family, and thus the rightful heir. Besides–'

Her aunt's reply was cut short by the sound of pounding feet behind them. Elisabeth saw John's body tense. She glanced around in time to see the two gentlemen who had been sitting on the bench now hurtling towards them. One threw himself at her aunt's guard, bowling the man over with the unexpected force of his attack. The other man stopped three yards from her side of the park bench and pointed a pistol at John's heart.

'Give me the bag now or you will die.'

John stepped forward, holding out the bag. From her side-on position, Elisabeth could see the taunt tendons in the man's trigger hand – he was going to shoot John, regardless.

She leapt to her feet, causing the man's aim to waver. 'I have the necklace.'

'No, I have it.' John waved the bag, drawing the man's attention back to himself.

The pistol swivelled from one to the other, before settling in her direction. 'Whoever has it will give it to me, or this young lady will be shot in her pretty little face.'

Elisabeth had never stared down the barrel of a gun, knowing that death was only a finger-twitch away. Her focus was drawn in to the small, black hole at the end of the barrel, as her peripheral vision and her courage shrank away. She forced herself to blink and refocus on the man's face – it was too late to change her plan now.

She signalled for John to stay back. 'If you will look away for a moment, please, I will retrieve the necklace from my boot.'

As she intended, the man only concentrated his attention more firmly on her. She lifted her foot to the end of the bench, as far away from her aunt as possible, and pulled her dress up to her knee. As she slowly unlaced her boot, she could see Palmer creeping closer to the other side of the man, his rake at the ready.

The end of the pistol dropped as the man watched her reach for the padded pouch, but it swung wildly up again when the knife appeared in her hand.

Before she had decided whether to throw the knife or lunge at the man, there was an explosion of movement in all directions. Palmer rushed in from one side, sweeping the rake upwards into the pistol-wielding arm. The man shrieked, and the pistol arced upwards as it went off with a deafening thunderclap.

Elisabeth dropped the knife and threw herself on top of her aunt, forcing them both down behind the minimal cover of the park bench. Out of the corner of her eye, she saw John's hat explode and his body drop to the ground. She screamed out his name, but heard no reply.

With a blood-curdling roar, honed by years as the mate of a sailing ship, Rivers raced the last few yards towards them, scattering his escort of ducks, and brought his cane down with a resounding crack on the head of the other assailant.

Palmer discarded his rake and charged like a battering ram, throwing the pistol man to the ground. They thrashed and rolled nearer and nearer to the edge of the water until the assailant somehow ended up on top, with a dagger in his hand. Blood dripped down its blade from the rake-marks on his forearm. Palmer's hand shot out to grip his wrist, forcing the knife away from his throat and eliciting a cry of pain from the assailant.

Elisabeth grabbed her own knife, but before she could rush to Mr Palmer's aid, she was halted in her tracks by a voice with all the authority of a battleground general.

'Stop!' her aunt commanded. 'Nobody will die over a piece of jewellery.'

The tableau of tangled bodies froze in place. Palmer took the opportunity to land a jaw-rattling punch, toppling his assailant. Elisabeth's racing heart jolted with relief, as she saw John push himself unsteadily to his knees.

Her aunt strode across to the man by the lake, who groggily raised unfocussed eyes towards her. 'You will tell your master that I never wish to hear from him again. He has maliciously destroyed everything I ever loved – my family, my friends, my home, my life. The necklace in that bag has been handed down through generations of women in my family, to my mother and now to me. He has no right to take that too.' She turned to John, who was now on his feet. 'Give it to me, please.'

John picked up the bag and handed it to her, as if mesmerised by the power in her voice. She reached inside the outer bag to touch the box inside, lifting the lid and sighing with pleasure at seeing the contents. She closed it, held it to her heart for a moment, then handed it back to John, kissing him on both cheeks and whispering in his ear. A smile spread slowly over his face and he bowed his head to her.

To Elisabeth's astonishment, John whirred the bag around his head and heaved it far out into the Serpentine, where it landed with a splash and sank into the dark water.

Elisabeth and both assailants screamed, 'No!' simultaneously.

'Tell your master that our family feud is now at an end. He must accept that, in this one endeavour, he has failed, as have I.'

Her aunt's imperious voice must have jolted her guard back to his senses. He jumped to his feet, dashed to her aunt's side and hauled her away down the path as fast as she could go. Her aunt turned, her mouth moving but no words escaping, as they disappeared around the corner into a dense stand of trees.

The guard's attacker was still on the ground, his body cowering under Mr Rivers' cane, though his eyes were fixed on the spreading ripples across the water. The pistol man was on his knees, staring at the spot where the necklace had vanished with the expression of a condemned man.

John picked up the pistol and hurled it into the water, then grabbed Elisabeth's arm. They raced back towards the carriage, with Palmer close behind them, while Rivers headed off in the opposite direction at a run. The two attackers stayed by the lake for several seconds, staring at the water, before recovering from their shock and giving chase.

When they reached the stand of trees, briefly out of sight of their pursuers, John jerked Elisabeth sideways, stopping behind the trunk of the largest tree, several yards off the path. Palmer raced on, yelling as if to urge them on, and drawing the attackers with him. John put his arms around her and pulled her to his chest. She slipped her arms around his waist, holding tight and listening to the pounding of his heart next to her ear, beating in counterpoint to the more distant pounding of feet.

They stood motionless until the only sounds were the breeze whispering through the autumn leaves and the peeps of the sparrows. Without saying a word, John wiped a tear from the corner of her eye and took her arm. The carriage was where they had left it, the driver napping in his seat in the sun, as if the violent ripples of the last half hour had dissipated, leaving only the calm surface of normality.

They travelled home in silence. Only when they were back in the warmth of the house, sitting in the library with tea and scones, did John turn to her with downcast eyes. 'Are you angry with me for throwing your family's priceless heirloom into the lake, as your aunt commanded?'

'I was shocked at first. But perhaps it is for the best. We will all be safer for it. More than anything, I am glad to have had the chance to talk to my aunt and grateful that you were there to protect us from harm. Bringing along Rivers and Palmer was a stroke of genius.'

The sound of the front door closing was followed by a thump of feet on the stairs. After a quick tap, the door opened and Rivers and Palmers entered the library. John sprang to his feet and bounded over to shake their hands.

'Thank goodness you're back. I was beginning to worry. Come and join us for tea.'

Both men hesitated, but Elisabeth handed out cups and gestured for them to sit. 'May I add my sincere thanks? You saved our lives.'

Rivers grinned at her. 'There's a bit o' life left in an old sea dog yet, eh, Miss Duval.'

'And everything went to plan,' added Palmer, 'more or less.'

Elisabeth was about to say, 'Apart from losing the necklace and nearly losing our lives', when she realised all three of the men had the same smug grin. 'Why do I feel like you all know something I don't?'

Rivers opened the bulky coat and handed her a bag identical to the one John had been carrying. She opened it, seeing, with astonishment, the jewellery box. She pulled the box out and opened it. The pearl necklace rested in its satin nest. 'Will someone please explain?'

'My apologies, Elisabeth,' John said. 'I was sure your aunt would be followed, so I took steps to lessen the risk. I was carrying an old cigar box filled with gravel. If the meeting had proceeded without incident, Mr Rivers was to come over at the last minute and substitute the real jewellery box.'

She looked around at the three chuckling men. 'Did you not think to include me in this plan?'

'I considered it,' John said, 'but I'm not sure even you could have acted the part quite so convincingly if you had known.' His grin faded. 'I'm sorry. I failed to take into account you ladies having plans of your own, although, I have to admit, you were both truly magnificent. Throwing the fake box into the lake was a brilliant idea, though for a minute there, I was worried you might jump in the lake after it.'

'Did you see the look on their faces? Priceless!' Mr Rivers chortled. 'They were certainly fooled, and I wager they'll not be bothering you again, Miss Duval. Their employer will not be best pleased.'

All three burst out laughing, this time joined by Elisabeth.

When Rivers and Palmer had departed, Elisabeth sat back on the settee and shook her head. 'You never cease to amaze me, Mr Godwin.'

'Long may that continue, Miss Duval. I could equally say the same thing about you. And your aunt. If I hadn't known better, I would have sworn she was looking at something of immense value when she opened that box of gravel. An impressive performance.'

'I hope you realise it was not the necklace I was worried about. For a terrible moment, I thought you had been shot.'

'A close call, I'll admit, and a ruined hat. Your trick with the boot and knife was quite a surprise too, although seeing that pistol pointing at you was the worst moment of my life. Next time, I will discuss the plan with you first, so you don't risk your life without cause.'

'Next time?' Fight and flight ebbed away and shock took over. Her body began to tremble of its own accord, as if deeply chilled, despite the warmth of the room.

'Elisabeth, it's over now and your aunt's enemies think the necklace is at the bottom of the lake. They won't be back.'

She pulled her cloak closer around her body and fought for control of her voice. 'The irony is that she had already decided I should keep the necklace, although I argued against it.' She paused and looked up at him. 'She also asked me to join her when she goes back to Europe.'

John's smile vanished. 'I was hoping you would stay here. I–.'

He was interrupted by another tap on the door. Mr Palmer handed over a message and closed the door behind him.

'It's from Mr Postlethwaite, for you.' John handed over a stained and tattered note, which had been enclosed within the note from the bookseller.

'It's from my mother.' She opened the letter eagerly, but her brief moment of joy faded as she read the hastily scrawled lines. Her face was white, and she was biting back tears by the time she handed the note back to him.

He sat down beside her and skimmed through the message. 'Your parents are safe. Surely that is good news?'

'Yes, but it is what they are not saying that worries me. Why are they still staying away from the farm and not telling me where they are?' Tears forced their way out and down her cheeks. 'They say it is not yet safe for me to return.'

He took her icy hands and warmed them between his own. 'The main thing is that your parents are alive and out of harm's way. We will send out messengers to track them down if we don't hear again soon.' He lifted her chin and wiped her tears away. 'You will see them again when all this dies down, I'm sure of it. Until then, you know you are welcome to stay here … if you choose to.'

She did not answer immediately, needing time to think through the conflicting demands on her heart. The desperate need to see with her own eyes that her parents were safe was tempered by the realisation that sending a messenger was the more sensible course of action. And though she would still like to find out more about her family, her aunt seemed as reluctant to talk about the past as her mother. And then there was the absolute certainty of what she felt for the man beside her, a rare and precious gift, given only to a lucky few.

His hands had dropped to his lap at her silence. His fingers fidgeted with the note. 'Did you see this postscript on the other side? "Belle is safe too and sends her love." Is Belle your sister?'

Elisabeth could not help but smile through her tears, that her mother knew her so well. 'Belle is my beloved horse. François will make sure she is looked after. I miss them all so much.'

His gaze fixed intently on her. 'When your aunt told me to throw the bag into the lake, she also said to tell you that you must keep the necklace as a wedding present. Is this François your betrothed?'

'No, my nephew.' She hesitated, knowing what she said next could change her life. 'My aunt may have got the wrong idea, seeing us together without a chaperone. She thought we looked … happy.'

He seized her hands again. 'I am happy when I'm with you. So much so that I can't imagine life without you. Elisabeth, I never knew love could feel like this.'

'Like pure joy, every time we are together, and torment to be apart?'

A smile lit up his face. 'You feel the same?'

'How could I not?'

He wrapped his arms around her and held her so close she could scarcely breathe. 'Marry me, my darling Elisabeth, so I need never be without you by my side.'

As had been the fate of generations of women in her family, the bitter salt of sorrow now mingled with tears of joy. She put her arms around his neck and gave her answer with a kiss.

Read on

Thank you for reading this novella.

If you enjoyed this book, I would be grateful if you could leave a rating or review to help other readers discover it.

The *French Legacy* story continues ...

Book 2, *The Widow's Secret,* recounts Elisabeth Godwin's voyage to New Zealand, trapped on a sailing ship, where social rivalries and ferocious storms are the least of her worries.

Book 3, *The Last Child At Versailles,* is a dual-timeline story, which reveals how the pearl necklace came into the possession of Elisabeth's family during the French Revolution and the ramifications for the family two centuries later.

Coming next ...

The *Penrose & Pyke Mystery* series is set during a remarkable period of social upheaval in 1890s

New Zealand. The stories feature Anne Godwin and the granddaughter of Elisabeth Duchamp Godwin.

Find out more at https://RosePascoe.com

Historical Note

France has fascinated me ever since I found out that my maternal grandmother's family originated there, before moving to England. We will never know what prompted a move between two countries that had so often been at war with each other, but it was enough to spark an idea for a story.

The characters in this book are entirely fictional, although it is set against a backdrop of historical events.

The few minutes of French history I was taught at school gave the impression that the French Revolution was a brief, if brutal, episode, centred around the storming of the Bastille. In reality, it was a much more drawn out and complex series of events. The revolution lasted a decade, between 1789 and 1799, but the turmoil in France continued for many decades after that, with a bewildering number of changes of regime.

During a turbulent half century, the fate of aristocratic families ebbed and flowed depending on their allegiances. Many lost their heads, while others lost their lands and fled to other countries, returning with each favourable change of regime to reclaim what they could. Of course, for most ordinary folk, no such option was available – they suffered hunger, deprivation and unimaginable bloodshed throughout.

In a nutshell, 1789 marked the fall of Louis XVI, of the Bourbon royal lineage, although he and his queen, Marie Antoinette, were not executed until 1793. A succession of populist leaders with increasingly ruthless agendas followed, with their brief turns in power often ending with their own necks under the guillotine. Napoleon seized power in the coup d'état of 1799, marking the end of the French Revolution.

Napoleon declared himself Emperor in 1804, until his defeat in 1814 led to the return of a king from the Bourbon line. Napoleon makes a brief reappearance again in 1815 for the 'Hundred Days', before the return of Bourbons. They ruled until 1830, when Charles X abdicated and the Duc d'Orléans seized power in the July Revolution. As Louis Philippe I, he was the last king of France, abdicating in the 1848 Revolution.

Acknowledgements

Many thanks to my friends and family for their support during my leap into the unknown.

I am very grateful to all the inspirational writers out there who encourage other writers, through teaching, speaking and blogging. In particular, I would like to thank three fabulous New Zealand writers for the generous gift of their time and expertise:
Mandy Hager (https://MandyHager.com), Diana Holmes (https://DianaKHolmes.com), and Leeanna Morgan (https://leeannamorgan.com).

Thanks also to Jenny Waters for her superb copyediting skills (https://redheadediting.co.nz).

About the Author

Rose Pascoe writes historical mysteries with a dash of romance, when she isn't plotting real-life adventures. She lives in beautiful New Zealand, land of beaches and mountains, where long walks provide the perfect conditions for dreaming up plots and fickle weather provides the incentive to sit down and write.

After a career in health, justice and social research, her passion is for stories set against a backdrop of social justice. Her heroines are ordinary women, who meet the challenges thrown at them with determination, ingenuity, courage, and humour.

Visit her at: https://RosePascoe.com

Other Books by Rose Pascoe

French Legacy series:
The Daughter's Promise
The Widow's Secret
The Last Child At Versailles

The Penrose & Pyke Mysteries
Murder in the Devil's Half Acre
Murder Most Melancholy
Murder By Vote
Murder in the Moonlight
Murder So Rash
Tinsel and Trickery
Murder Ignited
Murder Over Gold

www.ingramcontent.com/pod-product-compliance
Lightning Source LLC
Chambersburg PA
CBHW010932120626
46552CB00009B/3229